Lake Biwa Wishes

Judy Lussie

Sursum Corda Press, LLC

Cover Design by Chuck Eyler

Published by Sursum Corda Press, LLC
(sursumcordapress@comcast.net)

This novel's story and characters are fictitious. Certain long-standing institutions, agencies, and public offices are mentioned, but the characters involved are wholly imaginary. Any resemblance to actual persons, living or dead, or actual events is purely coincidental.

ISBN: 978-0-9799929-2-6 (paperback)
ISBN: 978-0-7999929-3-3 (e-book)
Library of Congress Control Number: 2016911459

To the three loves of my life:
My husband Bill, my sons Steven and Kevin,
who inspire me each and every day,
and to our many friends in Japan.

ACKNOWLEDGEMENTS

I want to thank my mentor, Julaina Kleist-Corwin, who convinced me to publish my stories. Also thanks to my critique group Sharon Burgess and Nate Hollingsworth, my beta readers Sherry Woodruff and George Cramer, my copy editor Violet Moore, and all my friends and colleagues in the Tri-Valley Branch of the California Writers Club. Without you, my stories would not have left my computer.

Lake Biwa Wishes

Judy Lussie

Lake Biwa Wishes

Chapter One

December 1976
Tokai-mura, Japan

Toni and her friends, Midori and Akiko, had just finished their high-impact aerobics session in the Tokai Community Center's all-purpose room. They walked through the corridor of the steel and glass building to get their winter jackets hanging on the coat racks across from a table of Ikebana floral arrangements. Toni thought the stoneware vase of three simple flowers was so elegant. She leaned over and sniffed the Christmas Camellia.

She looked up at the wall. "That poster wasn't there when we came in—must be something new." Still dressed in her exercise gear with her long hair rubber-banded into a ponytail, Toni pulled off her headband.

"It's an ad for a ski trip to Lake Biwa," Midori said. "I have an idea. Let's go skiing. I heard it's beautiful there."

Akiko leaned in closer to the picture. "Hmm…the scenery? Or the skier?"

Toni laughed at them. The three-foot poster promoting a Tokai Ski Club event featured a handsome skier schussing down a snowy slope.

Lake Biwa Wishes

Their teacher Ohno-sensei said, "I went last year and had a great time."

"Were the skiers this handsome?" asked Akiko.

Ohno-sensei giggled into her hand. "I met my fiancé there."

Sounds like fun. I don't need a fiancé, but it would be nice to be someone other than "mommy" or "wifey" for a weekend. Besides, I haven't been skiing since I left Idaho.

Toni Chang Morgan was living in Japan while her husband Greg was serving a two-year scientific exchange. People assumed she was Japanese—until she opened her mouth to speak. She constantly needed an interpreter.

Luckily she developed a friendship with Midori and Akiko. The trio were frequently together touring, taking doll-making classes and socializing with other Japanese friends. Although they spoke mostly English at first, their conversations evolved into a mish-mash of English/Japanese. Eventually Toni could speak Japanese without constantly consulting her language dictionary.

Toni queried Midori for more details about the ski trip. *This may be my chance to immerse myself into Japanese life.*

The three women walked to their favorite coffee shop down the street from the Community Center. Toni found the display of plastic food in the window fascinating. It was better than a menu. One could bring the waitress outside and point to a replica of the desired dessert. Everything looked amazingly appetizing. She decided to let her friends order the sweets.

"Coffee and cakes are our reward for working out," Toni said. She noticed Midori's wide grin. "I know...I know. I'm eating back the calories I just worked off."

Akiko said, "I love your American sense of humor."

While the waitress set tiny cups of espresso and a plate of pink and green tea cakes on their table, Toni said, "You know Keno-san from our doll-making class? Well, I went to her house for tea yesterday, and she had a new set of dishes. That woman is so lucky. I don't think I ever ate from the same china more than once in her house."

She noticed Midori eye Akiko with a smirk. "What's up?" Toni asked.

"Keno-san is not lucky. Just the

opposite," Akiko said. "She has new china because she throws them at her husband every time she finds out he had an affair with a woman."

Toni choked on her coffee. "Excuse me, did you say *an affair*?"

Akiko gingerly bit a piece of her cake. "Yes."

"Why does she put up with him?"

"Keno-san once told me he claims he loves her, but he also loves his mistress."

"Can a person love two people at the same time?" Toni asked as she shook her head.

She should kick him out, Toni thought. "Isn't divorce legal in Japan?"

"It is legal, but our culture does not condone divorce. Besides, Keno-san had an arranged marriage. Her mother-in-law keeps buying her new dishes and pottery and anything else breakable."

Toni kept her opinion to herself. *I wouldn't tolerate that from my husband. I would have an affair with another man.* Then she said, "I heard that some Japanese men have mistresses. Can't women have misters...or lovers?"

"Unfortunately, men who have mistresses are admired by other men. Women who have lovers on the side are shunned by other women and society."

Toni slowly exhaled. "The same double standard happens in America."

Midori, who had been silent so far, said, "When I was first married, love-making was wonderful. Then many years and three kids later, it got kind of boring. So now when we do our weekly thing, I imagine I'm with a handsome movie star."

Toni suppressed a giggle. She agreed with Midori, but her Japanese friends were extremely frank, open—like friends in her college days. "I think I'll try that," she said, glancing at the others to see if they would laugh. No reaction. Both women just stared into space.

I wonder what it would be like to have a fantasy lover, Toni thought. *Maybe I should try it sometime. But what if the fantasy turns out better than the real thing?* Toni cleared her head. *What am I thinking? I'm a happily married woman.*

Chapter Two

The next evening, Toni, Midori, and Akiko went to dinner with their families at the Golden Koi seafood restaurant. Midori had reserved a private room on the second floor in case the seven children, ranging in age from five to nine, were too noisy.

As they walked through the restaurant to the staircase, Danny, Toni's six-year-old said, "Look, Mommy. There's real fish swimming under the floor." He leaned closer to the transparent glass inset to view a stream of water with golden spotted koi. The other diners looked up when they heard English spoken. *Now they know we're gaijins.* Toni smiled and led her son away as other diners grinned and nodded at the Americans. The friends climbed a spiral staircase to their reserved private room where they sat on floor cushions at a long table, the adults across from each other at one end and children at the other.

Midori pulled out her tiny notebook held together with a gold elastic band. "I checked on the ski trip to Lake Biwa. The Tokai Ski Club is the official sponsor. The bus trip, lodging, food, and ski lessons are covered by one price." She looked up from her notes. "This is a very good deal. Participants must be members of the ski club, but since Toni-san is a foreign visitor, the trip coordinator said she would waive membership requirements. The only problem is that we can't take our kids."

Oh no. Babysitters, teenage or otherwise, are non-existent in Japan.

"If you want to go on the trip, I'll stay home with the boys," Greg said. "I can take off work Thursday and Friday and you'll be home by Sunday." He continued to reach for more sushi, dipping it in hot, spicy wasabi before popping it into his mouth.

"Thanks sweetheart," Toni said. Greg knew her so well, he could read her mind. They had been best friends since high school and married when she finished college. She smiled at her blond, blue-eyed husband. She was lucky, married to a renowned scientist.

Neither Midori nor Akiko's husbands said anything. Then Toni winked at Midori.

Midori said, "I want to go on the trip with Toni-san. She will need an interpreter."

"I have to work, not babysit," her husband Hiro Tanaka answered. "I'm not the American super-star scientist at our laboratory."

Greg put down his chopsticks for a moment. "Maybe we can use a little strategy. I'll tell our boss that I will not be in the office on Thursday and Friday so my wife can experience skiing with the Japanese Ski Club. Then you jump in saying that you also need to take off so your wife can accompany Toni whose Japanese is not very good. Our boss can't say yes to one employee and no to another for the same request." Greg helped

Lake Biwa Wishes

himself to another piece of *onigiri* sushi.

Akiko's husband, Ichiro Endo, laughed. He worked as an investment counselor for another company. "You are very clever, Morgan-san. If your scheme works, I will stay home with our children. I can work from my office or from my house."

"*Arigato.* Your heart is sweet also, my husband," Akiko added in English.

Toni breathed a sigh of relief. They were headed for a women's weekend without kids or husbands.

"Beware. There is a Lake Biwa myth about a dragon god who lives under the lake and will grant your wishes. However, the results may be good or bad," Ichiro said.

Chapter Three

Sunday afternoon, Midori, Akiko, and Toni entered the Community Center's large meeting room and joined the rest of the people with whom they were to spend the extended weekend. They helped themselves to refreshments of tea and Japanese sweets set on a long buffet table decorated with various *Bonsai* pine trees and framed photos of skiers. As the women sat in a row of chairs balancing paper plates filled with snacks, Toni glanced around the room. Most of the skiers were men. She was about to mention that fact to Midori, when three young women walked in.

They scanned the crowd, and headed toward the only other women in the room. "*Konnichi-wa. Inabe Harumi desu,*" the first woman said with a slight bow. The other two introduced themselves as Eiko and Mariko.

Midori waved her hand inward. "Please join us."

"Do you all speak English?" Toni asked.

"Yes," Harumi answered.

Toni let out a huge breath. "Great. I'm an American. My Japanese leaves a lot to be desired."

"I scanned the roster, and we are the only women on this ski trip," Eiko said as she took a bite of a jelly confection.

"Don't the men bring their wives or girlfriends?" Toni asked.

Harumi rolled her eyes. "Japanese men never take their wives on trips. If they take their girlfriends, they will have no privacy to..." The women all laughed before she finished.

When the coordinator read the room assignments, Toni understood the joke. All six women were to share one room. In fact, no one in their group had a single or double room. They were staying in a *Ryokan*, a traditional Japanese inn, not a western style hotel like Toni was used to.

"When I call your name, please state your age," the coordinator said, microphone in hand.

Lake Biwa Wishes

My age? I usually keep my age and weight private—sometimes I even lie. However, when in Japan, do as...

Her name was called. She said quietly, "*San ju.*" She observed that the men ranged in age from twenty to fifty. Toni and the other two housewives were in their thirties. The younger women were twenty-something. "Why do they want to know our age?" Toni asked.

"Age is important in the Japanese language which uses an honorific form of address," Akiko whispered back.

Chapter Four

Thursday, before the sun rose, Toni's husband pulled their car into the crowded parking lot of the Community Center. She could barely see through the thick exhaust from cars parked with the engines running. The air was cold that early in the morning. Toni huddled in her parka, blowing steam into the air while stamping her feet. She waved to her two friends. She hoped the chartered bus would be warm and comfortable.

She kissed her husband and her two little boys goodbye. While boarding the bus, she heard some whispers. "What is everyone whispering about?"

"You," Midori said, giggling.

"Huh?"

"You kissed your husband. Married women only kiss their children." Toni felt her cheeks flush. *Am I providing entertainment?*

Since it was still dark, most passengers had fallen asleep on the bus ride. Toni woke as the sun broke through the clouds peeking over the mountain tops. Other passengers stirred awake as the salty and sweet aroma of food filled the bus. Some of the passengers were opening their *bento* boxes. Toni had forgotten her packed lunch. She left it on the kitchen table in her house.

Midori reached into the overhead storage and brought down a box wrapped in a colorful square silk *furoshiki* printed with red and white roses. She unpacked the sushi makings, along with a thermos of fragrant tea. Then she showed Toni how to roll her sushi by taking a sheet of *nori*, rolling it into a cone and filling it with vinegar seasoned rice and pickled vegetables.

"Mine doesn't look as pretty as yours, but it sure tastes good," Toni said. She leaned back in her seat nibbling on her sushi. She wished she had the cold soy-sauced chicken she prepared the night before. *I hope Greg and the boys found it and ate it.* She prepared the chicken using an old Chinese recipe from her mother. It was times like this–traveling cross-country–that she got a lump in her throat thinking of her late parents, who always brought food on car trips.

Trying to lighten her thoughts, Toni asked, "How much further do we have to go?" She stopped and slowly slid down in her seat. She used to chide her kids for constantly chanting, "Are we there yet?"

"It is a nine-hour ride to Biwa Valley limits," a man turned around and answered in English. "If we get there soon enough, we might be able to have a ski run before the sun goes down. I hope you are enjoying yourself so far, Morgan-san."

"Yes. Thank you. I've never been in this part of Japan before. I love the beautiful view of Mount Fuji in the distance. The rolling hills are such a relief from the crowded cities."

Judy Lussie

She smiled. *I must still be hungry. Mount Fuji looks like it's topped with ice cream.*

Chapter Five

Lake Biwa, Japan

It was almost four o'clock when the bus entered another world, a village dipped in white. The snow was knee deep, and Toni felt homesick for Idaho where the only thing one could depend on was the white fluffy stuff in the winter—lots of it.

When she stepped off the bus, she did a

little dance in the deep snow making daisy print patterns with her boots like when she was a child. She looked up and realized that she was the entertainment again. The other passengers applauded when she stopped dancing. She held the hem of an imaginary skirt and curtsied.

"I can't wait to stay at a real *Ryokan*. So far I've only been in western style hotels since I've been in Japan," Toni said.

"Don't get your hopes up too high," Harumi said. "This is a ski lodge, not a luxury Ryokan like in the travel magazines." They picked up their ski gear and climbed the icy steps into the building.

Chapter Six

A kimono-clad hostess led the women to their quarters. They entered a large room with bleached beachwood walls, exposed beams, but no furniture. Japanese minimalism reflected the tranquility of the mountain area. The doors were sliding shoji screens painted with stylized landscapes of snow crusted pine trees.

Traditional Japanese futons were now

unfurled on the *tatami* mat floor to fit exactly six beds as tight as a Rubik's cube. Toni couldn't imagine that the six of them would be sleeping together on the floor.

When she and Midori shopped for bedding for the Morgan's company-owned house, Toni had learned that the top quilt was called a *kake-futon* and the mattress was called a *shiki-futon*. At the time, Greg suggested that she purchase a kake-futon large enough to use as a comforter on their king sized bed in Idaho. In the two weeks it took for the custom-made futon to be completed, they had to borrow a "two-person futon" from the Tanakas. Toni grinned remembering how much fun they had having sex on a Japanese futon. No worries about falling off the bed.

"Which futon do you choose, Toni-san?"

Midori asked, interrupting her reverie.

"As long as I get first choice, I'd like one in the middle, since I get cold."

"I like the one near the wall," Akiko said.

"I like to wake up and have the sun shine on me," Mariko said.

There was a knock on the door. *"Sumimasen..."* A kimono-clad hostess slid open the *shoji* door, bowed, set up a small wooden table and presented a tray of hot tea and *mochi*—a sticky sweet treat made from rice."

"Someone can have my *mochi*, I just want the tea," Toni said. Mariko, Harumi, and Midori did a Japanese version of "rock, scissors, paper" for the extra morsel. Toni offered a bemused smile. *The Japanese are too competitive.*

Three musical notes came over the intercom followed by a woman's voice announcing dinner in one hour. *"Wakarimas ka*–do you understand her?" Akiko asked.

"Hai," Toni said nodding her head. "I understand anything that has to do with food. I'd like to wash up before dinner."

"I'll go with you," Mariko volunteered. They consulted the map on the corridor wall and found the co-ed bathroom. When they walked into the bathroom, a man was using the urinal.

"Oh, excuse me," Toni said in English.

The man turned around and said, "Sumimasen," while he bowed twice with everything hanging out. Toni covered her eyes. When she sneaked a glance at Mariko, her face was expressionless. They left the bathroom without using the sink. When they turned the corner, Mariko burst out laughing. "He didn't even try to cover himself up." They giggled all the way back to their room.

"Are all Japanese men that immodest?" Toni asked.

"Only the old, ugly ones."

"What about the young handsome ones?" Toni quipped.

"I'm still waiting to see that." They both laughed.

"Are you married or have a boyfriend?" she asked Mariko.

"Neither, but there is one man I like. He is a ski instructor here. I convinced Harumi and Eiko to come skiing with this group so I could see him."

Toni noticed that Mariko was the prettiest of the young women. She was as tall as a fashion model, impeccably made-up, and brought the latest fashionable ski wear.

"The ski instructor is handsome. Rich. An Olympic champion," Mariko said as they entered their room. "I dream of being married to him and having his children... if that is ever possible."

"I can't wait to see what this guy looks like," Toni said. *Maybe he'll resemble my fantasy lover-to-be.*

Chapter Seven

Kenji Nakamura stopped on his way to Biwa Valley to put tire chains on his SUV. The snow was getting deeper, and he didn't want to get caught in a snow drift. Japan was not where he wanted to be right now. He had planned to be with his friends skiing and partying in St. Moritz. His mother had insisted that he return to Tokyo for his older brother's wedding. He liked his brother, but he and

Michio had never been very close. As the older Japanese son, Michio was their father's heir, expected to take over the family business and support their mother.

Nothing was expected of the second son, except to enter a profession, be self-supporting, and have a family. Now that Michio was to be married, Kenji's mother was determined to find him a wife. She probably had a line-up of single girls waiting for him at the wedding reception. Kenji felt lucky he found an excuse to ski. His cousin needed a ski instructor who could speak English for the Tokai Ski Club trip to the Biwa Valley since one of the skiers was an American who spoke very little Japanese. She had friends with her, but they still had trouble translating. As long as he was skiing, he wouldn't mind translating for some American housewife looking for a culture fix.

When he finally got to the Ryokan, it was too late to make a ski run. In fact, he would miss dinner if he didn't hurry. He registered, threw his gear into the room he was to share with the other two ski instructors, and walked to the dining room. The group was just finishing dinner, but the staff prepared a tray for him. He sat in the back and ate while watching a woman lead a sing-along.

She was doing a good job—everyone was singing *The Happy Wanderer* in English and clapping in time to the music. He figured she was one of the staff members.

As the waitresses began clearing the tables, Kenji looked at his watch. If he hurried, he could schedule a bath session. He checked with the bath attendant and reserved a half hour. These days he considered home to be Boulder, Colorado, but he missed some of the comforts of Japan, like a proper Japanese bath.

After a quick shower, he slowly stepped into the hot steamy pool. There was another man in the ten by ten foot wooden tub. The steam was so thick, Kenji didn't care if he knew the man or not. He remembered trying to describe a Japanese bath to Julie. She said, "You take a bath with people you don't even know?"

He explained it was like a hot tub without swimsuits. They got into a hot tub at a hotel in Aspen and took off their swim suits. But they ended up having sex right in the tub. That was not a proper Japanese bath. Kenji was surprised he still thought of Julie. They had broken up a month ago—out of boredom—at least on his part.

Kenji relaxed in the hot bath, letting all the cares of the day evaporate into the steam, until a buzzer sounded indicating that his time was up. He got out of the tub, rinsed off with cold water, put on a *yukata*, and walked back to his room. He heard several men shouting in Japanese, "We're going dancing with Morgan-san."

"Is Morgan-san the American? Is she a dancer? I thought she was a housewife," he said to Jun, his fellow instructor and roommate, when they were alone.

"She is a housewife," Jun said. "...but she's different. Pretty. Not frumpy." He sighed. "You have to see for yourself."

Chapter Eight

"What's that noise in the hallway?" Toni asked Harumi.

"The men want to go dancing tonight. They think you'll be there to dance with them. You became very popular after you sang for the group, Toni-san."

"What kind of dancing? Japanese folk dance?"

"No. Ballroom dancing. Or rock and

roll."

"Those old men like rock music?"

"Let's go to the dance," Mariko spoke up. "I saw that ski instructor. Maybe he'll be there."

"Okay. I want to see the guy you have a crush on."

"What is crush?" Mariko asked. "Should I dance and bump into him?"

"No. In America when you have a crush on someone, that means you like him but are too shy to say anything."

"That's Mariko," Harumi said. "She follows Nakamura-san everywhere."

"*Kenji Nakamura*, whose father owns the newspaper in Tokyo?" Akiko asked. "I read that he's an international playboy."

"*Hai*," Harumi said, nodding her head.

"Be careful of reaching beyond your grasp," Akiko warned in Japanese. "Wealthy playboys are nothing but trouble. You young girls go with Toni-san. I'll stay here and sleep. I am old and tired."

"I'm not old, but I am sleepy. I'll stay here too," Midori said.

Toni and the three young women entered the dining room which had been cleared and transformed into a dance floor. Only a few tables were left by the walls leaving room to dance. The lights were dimmed in an attempt to provide an ambiance of sort. A stereo connected to loudspeakers was in the corner.

Since there were only a few women, when the music played the men began to dance with each other. Toni tried hard not to giggle—she was unaccustomed to seeing men dance with men. "Do men always dance together in Japan?" she asked Harumi.

"Hai. Don't they in America?"

Toni didn't want to get into a discussion on homosexuality, so she just said, "Sometimes."

She Loves You by the Beatles came over the loudspeaker. "Morgan-san, please to dance with me?" asked a young man—the one who praised her leading a songfest. He said, "_The Happy Wanderer_ was the first record I ever bought with my own money." His remark made Toni feel ancient. Dancing with him made her feel closer to his age.

After the song ended, several men asked Toni to dance. She waved her hand in front of her face indicating she was tired.

She sat down next to Mariko and asked about the guy she liked. Mariko pointed to a man across the room talking to two others. He was handsome—tall, built like an athlete with coal black hair, longish at a time when most men wore crew cuts, and eyes that had a sad puppy dog look. "I see why you're attracted," she said to Mariko. "How do you let him know you like him?"

"I follow him everywhere and hope that he notices me."

She sighed. "Mariko, you've got to take the bull by the horns."

"Huh? Bull? Horns?"

"Let me show you. Watch..." she gestured with her hands to Mariko.

Toni walked toward the ski instructor

and waited for an introduction. The man standing next to him introduced him to Toni.

"*Komban wa,*" Toni said, bowing slightly.

"*Hajimemashite,*" Kenji replied.

"Do you speak English?"

"Hai, yes."

"My friend thinks you're really cute. She's dying to meet you."

Kenji's mouth curled into a slow grin. "That's a damn clever pick up line. Think I'll use it sometime."

"Oh my God, you speak American English. I'm so embarrassed."

"Oh, no. Are you the American housewife I was supposed to translate for? I was expecting someone more...you know... more Caucasian."

"I'm Chinese. I was born in Chicago. I look Japanese, so people think I can understand their language. If I don't understand and say *wakarimasan* they just speak louder."

KENJI COULDN'T HELP LAUGHING OUT LOUD. She was not only exceptionally good looking, she was amusing. "I don't think you look Japanese. You're much prettier," he said. *And sexier.* He fantasized about what she looked like under that bulky ski sweater. Beautiful and vibrant, she seemed like an Asian beauty, but her attitude was typical American. He wanted to wind his fingers through her waist length black hair, and his eyes fixated on that mouth that wouldn't stop talking. When she laughed, even her eyes sparkled.

"Well?"

"Well what?"

"Am I boring you? I asked you how you learned to speak English like an American. And forget the stories about being educated at Harvard before the war—I've seen the old Sussue Hayakawa movies."

He chuckled. "Actually, I graduated from Tokyo University and spent several years in graduate school at the University of Colorado. Boulder has been my home for ten years now."

"Did you come all the way to Japan just to translate for me?" she teased.

"I could lie and say yes, but my brother's getting married next week. I came back for the wedding." He signaled for a waitress to take his drink order. "Would you like a beer or *sake*?"

"Beer, please. Sake gets me drunk."

"Could be dangerous with all these men here."

"You're my translator. You'll protect me."

"That's a whole 'nuther skill set, ma'am. The fee increases," he said in a poor imitation of a Colorado local.

"Am I paying you?"

"Just for ski instruction—included in your package. So how much Japanese do you understand?"

"Mainly amenities and food stuff. I'm learning to read *katakana*. Next, I will try *hiragana*."

"Sounds aggressive and academic. Are

you dancing with all these men as cultural experiences, or are you looking for recreational 'you know what?'"

"I would never do 'you know what' with Japanese men. I've heard rumors about them," she whispered.

He furrowed his eyebrows. "Really? What did you hear?"

"In my *kima-komi* doll-making class, I heard that Japanese men weren't circumcised."

He wasn't sure if she was kidding or not. *Were they making voodoo dolls?*

"Are you Jewish?" he asked.

"No," she said with a slight wave of her hand. "It just seems kind of weird."

"We aren't any different from American men. I could show you my *ting-ting*."

The men standing around them

chuckled. She swatted his arm. *"Baka!"*

"I thought you didn't understand Japanese."

"That word I know. I have two little boys."

"But it had nothing to do with eating..."

"I'm not touching that remark with a ten-foot pole," she said. Kenji's face flushed a bright crimson which caused the men to laugh harder.

"Morgan-san is lots of fun," one man said in Japanese.

"Yeah. Like a barrel of monkeys," Kenji mumbled. "For that piece of humiliation, you owe me a dance." He pulled her to the dance floor.

They were slow dancing together. Kenji felt Toni melt into his arms. She was soft and comfortable. Too bad she was married. He didn't fool around with married women. He inched in closer and whispered in her ear, "So did you just make up that story about your friend?"

"Oh, I completely forgot about Mariko." She stopped dancing and led him away.

You jerk, he thought to himself. *When will you learn to keep your damn mouth shut? I loved dancing with her. She felt so good in my arms. Just my bum luck the friend was real.*

Toni pulled Kenji to where Mariko was sitting and introduced them. He bowed slightly, but Mariko just stared at him like she was in a trance. In the meantime, Eiko was talking to another man with her arms fluttering about. When she mentioned police, Toni's eyes lit up.

"What's Eiko talking about?"

"She was stopped by a cop and got a speeding ticket. She said if she was an American, she could have gotten away."

"Tell her I got a speeding ticket. Only women with long blond hair and big boobs get away with anything in Japan," Toni said.

All Kenji could think was *don't look at her chest. Don't look or you'll grow hard in front of her girlfriends.* He held his breath for a few seconds.

"Are you okay, Nakamura-san? You looked like you were going to faint."

"Guess I'm just tired. It was a long drive from Tokyo...and please, call me Ken. That's what my friends in America call me."

"Okay, Ken. You do look tired. Do you want to go to bed now?"

Lake Biwa Wishes

Why am I taking everything she says the wrong way? Of course I want to go to bed—with her.

Chapter Nine

Kenji Nakamura. Toni felt his heart beating when they danced. Her hands tingled when they touched. Maybe she had too much beer, because she couldn't possibly be infatuated over some man she had just met— no matter how handsome. Besides, she was a happily married woman.

As they walked back to their room, Toni ranted at Mariko. "I try to help you and end up making a fool of myself. When you met him, you didn't say a word. Now he thinks that I'm after him. Why do I always try to help people? I only end up getting in trouble."

Mariko looked at Toni dumbfounded.

"Harumi-san, please translate?" Toni said out of exasperation. Harumi translated while giggling.

"Shhh. You will wake up Akiko and Midori," Eiko said.

"We're already awake. The walls are thin. We heard you down the hall. What's going on?" Akiko said as she rolled on her side and braced herself on one arm. Midori stretched, rubbed her eyes and sat up. When Harumi explained in Japanese what had transpired, all the women started laughing. All except for Mariko, who hid from the group, tears streaming down her face.

Toni suddenly felt sorry that she was so pushy. It wasn't Mariko's fault. Japanese women were taught from childhood to be passive. She put her arm around Mariko to show she wasn't angry.

"Let's go to sleep. Breakfast will be at eight tomorrow," Harumi said. "Toni-san, fold your clothes and put them under your pillow. Then when you wake up they will be pressed and warm."

Hmm... The Japanese are very practical. She lay on her shike-futon and covered herself with the warm comforter. *I hope I don't dream about Mariko's playboy ski instructor. He's cute, but I have a husband. I can't wait to tell Greg about my adventurous day at the Ryokan. Maybe I should leave out the part about Ken.*

Chapter Ten

The next morning, the Tokai group gathered for a large Japanese-style breakfast in the communal dining room. They sat on cushions at long, low tables. Toni looked at the tray set before her and counted five separate dishes, each with a lid to keep the food warm. She didn't know if she was tempted by the aroma of her breakfast, but she was hungry. She lifted each cover and saw steaming white rice, miso soup, a colorful assortment of pickled vegetables artfully arranged into a still life composition, one whole grilled fish, and an egg. "Is this a hardboiled egg? It feels cold," Toni said. She started to crack it.

"Careful. It's a raw egg to break over your hot rice or miso soup," Harumi warned. Toni cracked the egg over her rice and replaced the lid. A few seconds later, it seeped into the rice and cooked. She sprinkled shredded, dried seaweed over the concoction.

"Delicious!" Toni didn't know how to eat the whole fish, so she observed other diners. The man sitting across from her bit off the head, then consumed the entire fish—bones and all. Toni decided to strip off the skin, debone the fish, and eat the flesh. She looked at the others around the table. No one even cared how she ate.

Toni assumed she would have time to digest her huge breakfast, but the coordinator announced that the shuttle bus was ready to take them to the ski hill. Luckily Harumi warned them to dress in their ski clothes before breakfast. They padded out to the *genkan* entryway in their stocking feet where their ski boots were waiting for them arranged according to their room numbers.

Metal binding cleats on ski boots clomping against the outer wooden walkway sounded like soldiers marching to war. Toni scanned the crowd for Kenji, but didn't see him.

When they got to the ski hill, there were other ski tours coming off shuttles. Flags were staked in the ground with the names of various tour groups. Toni recognized the Japanese *kanji* for Tokai and headed toward that flag. She waved to some of the men from the dance the night before.

The coordinator, equipped with a bullhorn, gathered the Tokai skiers. She asked a question and Harumi raised her hand and shouted, "I will interpret for Morgan-san." She winked at Toni. "We are instructed to take a test to assess our skill level. Any first time skier must step forward. They will be Team C," she explained to Toni. About eight people stepped forward, including Akiko, Midori, and Eiko. "The rest of you will have to take the test," Haruko interpreted to Toni in English.

Both Toni and Haruko were put into the intermediate class with two young men. Two others were assigned to the beginners' class.

The largest number of people, including Mariko, qualified for advanced.

Then three ski instructors schussed downhill with flourish. Snow crystals flew into the air like sparkling diamonds and fell softly on those gathered. Kenji skied to the intermediate class. He bowed.

"I assumed you were going to be with the advanced students," Toni said.

"I thought so, too, but Jun wanted the experience of leading more people, so he was assigned the advanced skiers. They're easier than beginners. Guess you're stuck with me," he said. "Besides, these two guys don't speak any English, so I'll have to give instructions in English and Japanese."

Kenji gathered his students into a huddle. "First, we must observe safety. Who has skied this run before?" he asked. "Okay, Takashi, you will be in the lead, and I will close up the end. We will *always* stay within sight of each other. I have never lost a student and don't intend to ruin my record. You're in the intermediate class because each of you mastered the snowplow turn. After you become accustomed to more speed, the Stem Christie is the next turn to accomplish. I'll have you parallel skiing downhill like an advanced skier in no time. Now watch me do a Stem Christie."

Kenji was an excellent instructor. Each student practiced the turn he demonstrated. Toni already knew how to do a Stem Christie, but she let him hold on to her waist as he straddled her skis and turned with her. Their bodies were so close together, they moved as one. When she edged her ski into the snow, she turned to look at him and almost kissed him. The scent of his cologne on her jacket gave her a giddy feeling in the pit of her stomach. *What's going on? I feel like a teenager again.*

Kenji sucked in his breath and said, "Keep your eyes focused on where you're going."

He did not double ski with the other students but watched their form standing downhill. "Okay, now we're ready for steeper hills and more speed. But first let's stop for lunch. This time I'll lead and Takashi-san will close up."

They skied downhill when suddenly Takashi shouted in Japanese, *"Nakamura-sensei! Wait. Morgan-san fell down."*

Kenji climbed back uphill as Toni got

upright. "I'm okay. I just hit a soft patch." She brushed the snow off.

"Are you sure?" he said as he felt the inside of her lower leg. She felt lightheaded when he touched her, even through her thick ski pants. *What's the matter with me? I should slap him if his hands get any higher.*

"I've fallen down before," she said. "No big deal. Anyway, I'm hungry."

"Okay, follow me. The *soba-ya* is beyond that hill."

They stopped at a little soba restaurant which only served noodles prepared in various styles. Toni thought it was charming. The wooden post and lintel structure with a sloped roof over the entrance and paper windows looked like a building out of an old samurai movie. The only indication it was an eatery was the *noren* or curtain over the doorway which brushed her head as she entered. Once inside, she inhaled the fragrant scent of sweet soy sauce and ginger. There were no vacant tables large enough for the five of them. Harumi and Takashi quickly took a table for two. Toni sat down at another table for two, which left Satoshi, the other student, to decide where to sit. Kenji pulled up a chair and invited Satoshi to sit with him and Toni.

"No speak *Eigo*," Satoshi said waving his hand in front of his mouth.

"*Daijobu*," Toni said, assuring him she was okay.

"So, tell me. Why did you pretend you couldn't do a Stem Christie?" Kenji asked in English.

Toni shrugged. "Maybe I wanted you to

show me how, properly. Actually, I could never qualify for the advanced class. I'm terrified of moguls."

"Snow mounds? Or rich men?"

"Which are you?"

"Neither. My father and brother are rich. I'm not."

Toni remembered Akiko's warning of Kenji Nakamura being an international playboy. "...and you'd probably melt the snow mounds—you're so hot. You're cute, but conceited as hell."

"I am not. Besides, you're just a prick teaser," he mumbled under his breath.

"I. Heard. That." Toni squinted her eyes. "Is trash talk part of your womanizer pick-up line? If so, it's not very romantic."

"Sorry. I don't usually call anyone a PT,

but I'm not a womanizer. I'm a one-woman man," he said, as the waiter set steaming bowls of soba noodles on their table.

"Where's your one woman now? In Japan or Colorado?"

"Nowhere. We broke up a month ago."

Toni took chopsticks out of the *ohashi* holder and slurped up a mouth full of noodles. "How come?"

"My God, has anyone ever told you you're nosy as hell? How is this any of your business?"

"I like to solve puzzles. So far, I figured you almost ravished me on the dance floor last night because you're horny and on the rebound."

"So now I'm not only conceited, I'm a molester? You're still a PT," he sneered.

Toni was suddenly aware of Satoshi sitting with them quietly eating his soba. "Are you sure he doesn't understand what we're saying?"

"Maybe he has a tape recorder hidden in his pocket and is planning to blackmail the both of us," Kenji whispered. Toni giggled, covering her mouth with her hand.

"Good grief, I'm doing the Japanese female thing. By the time I leave Japan, I'll probably speak in a high octave sing-song voice."

This time Kenji laughed. "You might be a PT, but I think you're pretty funny."

"Funny ha-ha or funny looking?"

"Definitely not funny looking," he said with a mischievous grin.

"Let's change the subject. Why did you

break up with 'One-Woman-san,' or did she dump you?"

"We parted as friends. Got bored with each other. Only thing we had in common was sex. I felt like the resident bull who was servicing her." He looked up at Toni rolling her eyes. "That doesn't mean I'm conceited."

"Are you gay?"

"I've told you too much already. You should work for the American CIA. You have all the attributes for a spy. Time to get back to skiing." He waved to the other students.

Chapter Eleven

They skied downhill, practicing their Stem Christies. Then Kenji explained he was moving them into parallel skiing. Toni was afraid of the speed needed to do parallel turns. She kept falling down, as did the other three students. "Nakamura-sensei! Are you torturing me because I asked if you were gay? I really don't care. It's none of my business."

"I'm not gay. And I am not torturing

you. You have to practice to learn, and falling down is part of the practice. Skiing requires speed. Don't fear it. Feeling the wind in your face is almost erotic." He looked directly into Toni's eyes.

She hoped what she was feeling was not eroticism. They were on a cold ski hill, and she was sore from falling down so often. But a warm tingling coursed through her body whenever he looked at her.

They skied to another ski lift to go higher up the mountain. When they each skied off their lift chair, they followed Kenji to a viewing area. "This is why people like to ski at this resort," he said. They were treated to an expansive panorama of the valley below including a magical vista of Lake Biwa. Little hotels and Ryokans surrounded the lake like a miniature village. "A *biwa* is a Japanese lute—like the shape of this lake. It's so large you can only see the entire lake from an airplane." He looked at Toni. "You won't see a view like this if you only ski the bunny hills. You have to move out of your comfort zone—spread your wings, so to speak."

"What a breathtaking view. I could stay here forever. Arigato, Ken. I'm sorry to be such a pain in the neck."

KENJI LOOKED AT HER. *That's not the part of my anatomy that's in pain. You're starting to affect my heart. Too bad you're married.* "Lake Biwa is also credited with having magical powers," he said, trying to regain his composure. "Once when I was a child, my mother brought me skiing here. I was upset about something, so she suggested I make a wish to the Dragon God living under this lake."

"What did you wish for?" Toni asked. "Did it come true?

"I wished to be the greatest skier in the world."

Toni clapped her mitten covered hands. "See, it came true. You have several Olympic medals." She looked up at him. "Do you think if I make a wish it'll be granted?"

He shrugged. "It's something parents tell children."

She closed her eyes and screwed up her face. Then she took a deep breath. "Done."

Kenji laughed. He enjoyed her childlike antics. "What did you wish for?"

Toni shook her head. "Can't tell what

my wish is or it won't come true."

They began to descend the hill, when he said, "We're pretty high up the mountain. This is considered an advanced trail. You can still make it around the moguls if you're careful. Don't worry, I'll be watching you."

The five skiers made it to the bottom of the hill, stopping often to keep the group together. When they stopped at the Tokai flag, they cheered themselves, shouting "B, B, B!"

Kenji was proud of his students' first day, but one student captured his attention, as she winked at him and mouthed "Thank you."

He blushed, reminding himself again that she was a married woman with children. He had no respect for married people who played around, but he couldn't stop thinking about her. He liked the way she looked, how she felt in his arms when they skied. He promised himself to practice a lot more self-control.

Chapter Twelve

The shuttle bus dropped tired skiers off at the Ryokan. Toni couldn't believe she had skied for a total of seven continuous hours. She only took a half hour off for lunch. "I am so sore," she said. "Every inch of my body hurts."

"I fell down so many times, I could have skied on my seat," Midori said.

When they entered their room, the futons were rolled up and stored, so sitting on the hard floor was cold. They huddled around a kerosene space heater in the corner of the room. Just then Akiko walked in.

"I made a reservation for us to use the bath. It only holds four, so Midori, Toni and I will take a half hour, and Mariko, Eiko, and Harumi will take the second half hour."

Toni had never been in a public bath before but had read all about the etiquette, so she eagerly anticipated the new experience. The company house her family lived in had a wooden *o-furo*, but because they were Americans, the deep wooden tub was replaced with a shiny new porcelain bathtub.

As they walked to the bath, they passed a man who had obviously just finished bathing. He was walking down the hall completely naked with his *yukata* and towel around his neck. Steam still emanated from his body. Akiko shook her head. "He was never taught proper manners." Toni could feel the heat crawling up the back of her neck. The only naked males she saw were her sons and, of course, her husband. She couldn't wait to tell Greg about how the men in Japan were so immodest.

The three women walked to the bath and signed in with the attendant who issued each of them a cotton *yukata* and towels. When they walked into the bath, the first thing Midori did was to drain the tub. Then Akiko took a bottle of Clorox and a brush and scrubbed the inside of the tub and rinsed and refilled it with hot steamy water.

"Do you always do this?" Toni asked.

Midori giggled. "Of course. I don't want

the germs of strange men to contaminate my bath. We always scour the bathtub—we're not at home." The two women offered the first soak to Toni out of respect to her being the guest. Then they went into the outer room to wait. "Don't forget. Only soak for ten minutes, or you will get a headache," Midori shouted.

Toni showered with the soap and warm water, then slowly stepped into the tub, letting the water rise up to her chin. The bath reminded her of how her mother cooked lobsters by dropping the live crustaceans into boiling water. She could feel all her aches and pains from the vigorous day of skiing melt into the steamy water. When her timer sounded, she rinsed off and put on her cotton yukata. She didn't know whether to drain the large tub or not. Midori and Akiko came in and told her to leave the water in. "We know you don't have germs," Midori said.

Toni walked back to her room alone while Midori and Akiko enjoyed their bath. She saw Kenji walking toward her. She didn't know whether to acknowledge him or not. She could not avoid him. She was underdressed in her thin yukata with her clothes folded in her arms. Besides being cold, she felt so exposed. They nodded to each other. She walked quickly to her room and wasn't aware of him turning around to watch her.

HE THOUGHT, WHY DOES THIS woman fascinate me? She looks just as good from the back as from the front, even wearing a frumpy yukata. It's not like she's available. She has a husband and two kids. *Restrain yourself, Kenji, old boy. You do not fool around with married women—especially one with two sons.* He remembered the hell his father had put his mother through when she found out he had a mistress. That was probably the reason Kenji swore he would never get married.

TONI GOT TO HER ROOM and looked at herself in Mariko's mirror. Wearing no make-up these days, Toni prided herself as a liberated woman. She kept her long, straight hair waist length. Mariko, on the other hand, looked glamorous, even though Midori and Akiko made fun of her behind her back. Akiko referred to her as the painted lady. When Mariko unpacked her belongings, Midori said in English, "Your hobby must be cosmetics."

Toni tried to fix up Mariko with Kenji, but as pretty as Mariko was, he wasn't interested. Toni decided to mind her own business from now on. She was beginning to feel flattered by Kenji's attention.

She dressed in her favorite ski sweater and jeans for dinner. She put on heavy socks so she wouldn't have to walk in the hotel slippers which were too big. Just then, Midori and Akiko walked into the room. "I feel so much better after soaking in the bath," Akiko said. "Too bad it's too cold to eat dinner in our yukatas."

Chapter Thirteen

In the dining room, they were sitting at a long dinner table when the instructors came in. Kenji bowed as the skiers greeted him with "*Komban-wa, sensei.*"

"*Komban-wa, mina-san,*" he replied to the group.

Still feeling sore from the day of vigorous skiing, Toni greeted him with a sneer saying, "*Komban-wa,* torturous teacher."

He replied "Komban-wa, PT-san," with a half grin.

Toni was about to get angry, when Midori asked, "PT means what?"

Akiko quickly answered in Japanese, "Petite means small." She gestured with her palms slowly moving toward each other. "Toni-san is tiny."

"_Ah so,_" Midori said. The people within earshot repeated the understanding with their hands gesturing in imitation of Akiko. Toni had been unaware that people at their table were listening to them. She looked at Kenji, and they both burst out laughing.

"Sorry about the name calling," he said. "I was acting petty and childish."

"Me too," Toni said. "I probably started it."

Lake Biwa Wishes

"Truce?"

"Yes."

"Friends?"

"Definitely," Toni said as she and Kenji did a high five. She heard people at their table doing the same, shouting "Friend" in English or *Otomadachi* in Japanese. She imagined she could spread world peace like this.

Then Kenji stood with his glass of beer in hand and congratulated Team B for the progress they had made. Takashi stood and attributed their success to their teacher. The team stood and shouted "B, B, B!" As each team did the same, the response got louder and louder. So many people were in Team A, their cheering was deafening. Toni covered her ears with her hands.

"I'm having so much fun. Thanks,

Ken...for teaching and translating," she quickly added.

"I aim to please," he said.

"Oh look, they're bringing out the karaoke machine," Toni said. A man brought a book to Toni and said something to Kenji to translate.

"He found some songs with English lyrics. He wants you to sing." Toni flipped through the catalog and found the perfect song. In the meantime, one man was singing a Japanese song dedicated to her. After he ended, she bowed slightly and whispered "*Domo-arigato*" in thanks.

It was Toni's turn. She took the printed lyrics, walked up to the microphone, and sang to a taped accompaniment of *Top of the World*. When she sat back down, she said to Kenji,

Lake Biwa Wishes

"That was for you. You showed me Lake Biwa and cured my fear of moguls."

"That's the nicest thing anyone ever said to me. You have a beautiful voice, Toni. I still can't figure how you can sing in front of a large crowd and be afraid of skiing fast."

"Speed kills, singing doesn't."

"If I sang in front of a crowd, they'd all want to kill me."

"Don't put yourself down, Ken. It ruins your conceited image," she teased.

"I thought we had a truce," he said. Then he got up to say something to Takashi.

"What did you say to him?"

"It's a surprise for you."

Toni enjoyed surprises, so she sat and patiently waited. Takashi took the microphone and sang the *Hawaiian Wedding Song*. While

Takashi was singing, Kenji fixed his gaze on her. She looked into his eyes and felt tingling down to her toes. She was afraid of attracting attention. When she looked at Takashi his focus was directed to Harumi. No one even looked at her or Kenji. Takashi and Harumi must be falling in love.

"Did you know they were becoming a couple?"

"Yeah. It was hard keeping them with the group. I let them be alone as much as safely possible," Kenji said.

"What about you and Mariko?"

"There is no me and Mariko. She's what my mother would call a 'gold-digger.' She's not interested in me. She wants to marry into a wealthy family. And don't call me conceited. This is how life is in Japan."

Lake Biwa Wishes

Toni said nothing. She was beginning to realize that Kenji was a nice man. She drank the rest of her beer and set her glass down. He refilled it. Toni took the large bottle of Kirin and filled Kenji's glass, saying "One thing I learned is that you should never pour your own drink. Friends pour for each other."

"Here's to you, my friend. *Kampai*," he said as he toasted her. They clinked their glasses.

"I never used to drink beer. Since I've been in Japan, I drink it all the time," Toni said after she took another sip.

"Maybe I can get you drunk enough to take advantage of you," he teased.

"In a room with five other women?"

"Never tried it with six women—I'd probably be dead by morning."

"Why? Are you going to sing too?"

"Okay. You got me." Kenji chuckled. He downed the rest of his beer. "Wanna go to the Ryokan next door to see a hokey geisha show?"

"I'd love to. I never saw a geisha before. Why is it hokey?"

"The dancers are local girls in kimonos. Not at all like the real geishas in Kyoto. Let me see if your girlfriends want to go."

Kenji, Takashi, and Satoshi escorted the six women to the geisha show. "This is weird. Usually groups consist of one woman for every two men. I feel like a tour leader," Kenji said.

"You are. All you're missing is your flag and bullhorn."

He laughed. Toni enjoyed making him laugh. They were beginning to become comfortable with each other. Like old friends.

They walked into a smoke-filled bar with a wooden dance floor which reminded Toni of a Japanese version of the cowboy bars in Idaho. It even smelled like a cowboy bar — old wood and dead beer. The men were groping kimono clad women who resembled hookers with their kimonos askew. She recognized one man from the Tokai tour group who turned away embarrassed when he noticed them.

Takashi found a table large enough for nine in the back of the room. As they sat on the cushions, the lights dimmed and a spotlight focused on a makeshift stage. The dancers paraded out with hoots and howls from the audience. Midori began giggling into her hand. "They're terrible. I think some of them are drunk."

"I always wondered why my husband goes to bars like this. Seems disgusting," Akiko said. Toni was shocked. *Akiko's serious, intellectual husband frequented bars?* She was just about to say something when she glanced at Kenji who shook his head with a frown.

"Don't say anything. You're in Japan. Accept our values here," he whispered as he downed his beer. Until he said that, Toni had thought of Kenji as just another American. She had forgotten he was Japanese first. He must be more complex than she assumed.

Chapter Fourteen

The next morning they got up at the sound of three musical notes. Toni looked toward the window. The sun had barely risen. She had learned how to keep her clothes with her under her pillow. She didn't throw off her comforter until she put on her sweater, pants and socks over the long underwear she wore to sleep. She was so cold she would have worn her ski coveralls and gloves, except they hindered her mobility.

Mariko rose earlier than the others to have time to apply her make-up. She looked beautiful, but inappropriate for sports. She didn't say a word.

Toni tried to lighten up the tension in the room. She turned to Harumi and said, "So are you and Takashi going to see each other after we get back to Tokai?"

Harumi blushed. "Yes. I live in Hitachi City and he lives in the laboratory's dormitory in Tokai. He asked if he could visit me."

Midori, Akiko, and Eiko oohed and aahed. Toni noticed that Mariko didn't respond, but continued brushing her hair in silence. Toni felt like she had stolen Mariko's boyfriend, but some men just appreciated personality more than beauty. Besides, in no way was Toni on the prowl for any man. She was happily married.

When they sat down to breakfast that morning, the meal was similar to the day before, except the fish was a grilled fillet instead of a whole fish. The dish of *takuan* pickles had grated white *daikon* radish and thin strips of pickled green peppers arranged to look like a snow capped mountain with pine trees. "Oh, the takuan is too beautiful to eat," Toni said.

"First you feast with your eyes, then you savor with your mouth," Midori said.

KENJI ENTERED THE DINING ROOM and decided to sit and socialize with skiers other than Toni. He had difficulty maintaining his composure around her. She either riled him with her smart mouth, or drove him crazy with her sex appeal.

Takashi stopped him and said, "Please sit here with us, *Sensei*. You need to translate for Morgan-san."

"Were you trying to avoid me, *Sensei*? I thought we were friends now," she said with a coquettish tilt of her head.

"It's just that I can't figure you out. One minute you're a..." he had to avoid saying PT again "...you know what, next you're doing something nice like singing *Sakura* in Japanese. You made a big hit last night. They'll probably elect you mayor of Tokai."

"And I can't figure out if you're insulting or flattering me," she said.

Grinning, Kenji finished eating and

looked at his watch. "It's time to hit the slopes. *Ikemashio!*" His students dutifully followed him out to the waiting bus.

Chapter Fifteen

When the shuttle dropped the skiers off at the ski hill, Akiko commented, "The sun is not out today. It may snow."

"We would have nothing to ski on if it didn't snow," Midori said.

Group B followed their instructor to the chair lift. They were going to ski down a more advanced hill. Toni hoped she would experience another view of Lake Biwa from the top of this mountain. By the time they got off their chairs, it was snowing harder. Toni noticed the lifts were still running, so they probably expected the snow to slow down.

As they waited for their group to get off the chairs, the wind began to blow harder. Toni stopped to remove her goggles and wiped off the snow, but ended up getting more snow inside them and in her eyes. Looking through her wet lenses, she couldn't see where she was going. *Which direction is the fall line?* She panicked. Kenji was shouting instructions, but with the wind blowing, she couldn't hear what he was saying. *Was he speaking English or Japanese?* In her disorientation, Toni fell. Her bindings did not automatically release and she tumbled head over heels with her skis still attached.

Judy Lussie

KENJI'S HEART JUMPED INTO HIS THROAT when he saw her fall. He was responsible for these people. If anyone got hurt, it would have been his fault for pushing them too hard. He shouted in Japanese, "You three stick together. Hold onto each other's clothes or ski poles. Further down the hill there's a shelter. When you get there, stick your ski upright in the snow and attach this Tokai flag. Then the ski patrol will be able to spot you after the blizzard calms. In the meantime, help put Morgan-san on my back. With the extra weight, I'll have to ski slowly. Meet you at the shelter. *Ikemashio.*"

"Ken, I'm scared and my leg hurts like hell." She rode piggy-back with her skis attached swinging loose on either side of him.

Lake Biwa Wishes

"Don't worry I'll take care of you. Hang on tight. I've rescued people before."

When they got to the shelter, Kenji didn't see the Tokai flag. His heart thumped faster. He kicked open the door, and stood in the genkan, looking around. He had never been to this particular shelter before, but it was no different from the others. A musty-smelling wood cabin with a fireplace. The full-length sliding glass windows were boarded up, putting the entire interior in darkness. He needed to let in some light, but he had to deal with Toni first.

Toni was getting heavy on his back. "Which is your good leg? I'll release your bindings by hand if you can jump down." Toni jumped down on her right leg and fell on the floor moaning in pain while he got her bindings and boots off.

He unzipped the left leg of her coverall and felt for broken bones. "I think you just have a misaligned knee. Hope it's not broken. Breathe in and out slowly," he said as he rubbed her leg, then he snapped it into place. Toni let forth an ear shattering scream. Then she felt nothing.

"What did you do? Perform a miracle? My leg feels fine," she said.

"Thank goodness it wasn't broken."

He took his ski and stuck it upright in the snow outside attaching a Tokai flag to it. The snow was deeper than when they arrived. He slid open the wooden shutter of one window to let in some light. "I'm worried sick about Takashi, Harumi and Satori. They were supposed to be here by now." He opened and slammed cabinet doors until he found a short-wave radio with earphones. "CQ, CQ," he shouted into the microphone. "*Hai, dozo, hai, dozo,*" he said after a long minute.

He watched Toni walk across the room on her newly healed leg. "Ken, you're better than a doctor," she said.

He turned off the radio and faced Toni. "Are you okay now?

"Yes. You're a miracle worker. What's the latest news on my classmates?"

"Command post has no report on them. The snow storm is too heavy to do a ski patrol search. I just hope they found a cave or shelter." He pulled off his ski cap and ran his fingers through his damp hair. Tears were running down his face.

Toni put both hands on his shoulders.

"Don't worry Ken. You healed my leg. I have faith in you. You can do anything."

He looked into her eyes. She was so tempting. But he had things to do. He found some firewood in a bin by the fireplace and started a fire. "The chimney smoke should alert rescuers that we're here. They'll see the smoke before the flag," he said. "Come, warm yourself. Toni, your clothes are soaking wet."

"That's because I kept the snow off your back."

"True," he agreed. "Take off your wet clothes and let them dry by the fire." They both took off their jackets, hats, gloves, and coveralls and lined them on the floor in front of the fireplace.

"I feel like I'm playing strip poker without cards."

Lake Biwa Wishes

"Are you a good poker player?"

"Of course."

"Remind me not to play cards with you."

"You did offer to show me your *ting ting*..." she said. He raised one eyebrow, so she quickly added, "I'm just kidding."

"Like you want something to tease it again?" He was standing very close to her—kissing distance—when the radio screeched. He ran to the radio and put on the headphones. *"Hai, hai..."* He took off his earphones and breathed a sigh of relief.

"What's the news?"

"That was Takashi. Thankfully, the three of them made it to the bottom of the hill. They were hanging on to each other. Blinded by the blizzard, they saw no house or shelter.

We're the ones lost in the snow. The chair lifts shut down as the last of the skiers got off. As long as we're safe and warm in this shelter, no one will search for us until the snow stops," he said.

"How long are we stuck here for?"

Kenji shrugged his shoulders. "We'll have to make the best of it. If you get hungry, maybe we can find a stash of emergency tea and packaged ramen noodles. But, there's no western style bathroom.

"That's okay, I've gone camping before. Besides, we live in a company house with a Japanese toilet room. My husband converted it to meet our personal needs."

"Really? I'm surprised the Japanese government didn't modernize your house suitable for gaijins."

She shrugged her shoulders. "We didn't want special treatment. We're not ugly Americans."

"That's commendable," he nodded. "In the meantime, we've got to conserve heat until our clothes dry." He pulled a large futon out of one of the cabinets and shook it out.

"Are we going to sleep?"

"No, we're going to keep warm with our body heat. You still don't trust me?"

"I trust you." She looked at him with her eyes wide, like she was frightened.

Kenji proceeded to lay the futon on the floor and placed the comforter on top. "Ladies first," he said as he folded down the kake-futon.

"Is it clean?"

"Probably not, although I didn't see any

mice droppings."

"I'm not getting in that dirty futon."

"Suit yourself, I'm cold." He got in and pulled the coverlet up to his chin. She stamped her stocking feet while holding her arms across her chest to keep warm. After a few minutes, she looked down at him.

"Okay Ken, move over, I'm coming in. Just don't try anything. I take karate classes."

"*Dozo gozaimasu,*" he said as he lifted the top quilt for her.

Chapter Sixteen

Toni got into the futon with him and lay there, stiff as a wooden soldier. She didn't know if she was still cold or just nervous being so close to a man not her husband. Her chest tightened. She'd never been in bed with another man, but Kenji was so tempting. Handsome. Warm. Hot, actually.

He put one arm around her. "You're still cold. Move in closer."

Judy Lussie

She had to admit it felt good being close to a warm body. She sometimes had fantasies about being with another man, but this was real. Without realizing it, she blurted out, "What am I supposed to do? Sleep or what?"

"Anything you want. Why don't you sing a song?"

"Lying down?"

"Stand up if you want."

Thinking it would calm her anxiety, she started singing her favorite Karen Carpenter song in her breathy voice. When she got to the part, *"Just like me, they long to be close to you,"* Kenji pulled Toni close and kissed her.

"I wanted to do that from the first time I saw you." He looked into her eyes with that sad puppy dog expression. She knew she should pull away from him, but she just lay there. He ran his hand along her curves, nibbling on her ear. "I think I'm falling for you. I never felt like this with any other woman before."

She had no smart comeback. This was probably one of his playboy womanizing lines, but she didn't want to leave his warm body. She squeezed in closer. She enjoyed his kiss. Any previous guilt she felt melted in the heat of passion. She ran her finger down his nose and across his lips. He opened his mouth and captured her finger. Suddenly she seemed to regain her senses.

"What if we don't get rescued? What if we run out of firewood? We could die of hunger or freeze to death," she said as she snuggled up against him.

"I'm Japanese. I accept the inevitable. If

we die here together, I'll die in peace."

"Well, I'm American. I don't want to die, and I'm scared."

"_Toni-chan_, don't worry. I'll take care of you." I think I love you, he thought.

"..._chan?_" she said. "Isn't that how you address children?

"It means Toni baby." She looked at him with conflicted emotions while she nestled in closer, their bodies almost as one.

"Have you been stranded in blizzards before?"

"Yup. In Gstaad, we were trapped in a shelter for three days."

"Did you have a woman with you then too?"

"One woman and two other men. We took turns with her. Nine month later, when she discovered who her baby's father was…"

"*Baka!* You made that all up."

"You almost believed me. Actually, I was with two other men. We drove each other crazy in three days. This is the first time I've been trapped with a beautiful girl. I could enjoy this if I wasn't so damn cold. Kiss me again—maybe I'll warm up."

She giggled. "Kissing doesn't make you warm."

"With the right woman it does. Didn't you ever hear about magic kisses? Kiss one—we're in another time and place. Kiss two—you're not someone else's wife. Kiss three—you love me as much as I love you…"

"Wait. You're moving too fast. We only met two days ago. You don't know anything about me."

Judy Lussie

"I know that you are the most difficult woman to get along with, but for some reason I keep coming back for more abuse. And you have a dual personality—one minute you're smart-mouthing people with insults, the next, you sing songs to make them adore you."

"What about you? You parade into a room like God's gift to women. You look down on women who admire you in favor of someone you can't have just to prove your virility. You pretend to be tough on the outside, but break into tears if a friend is in danger."

"I forgot to mention you're a pseudo psychoanalyst. And I still haven't kicked you out of our dirty futon."

"Does that make you a masochist? I'm not into that kind of perversion."

He rolled on top of her. "The only thing I want to be into is you—and that's not perversion."

"Ken, please don't make me want you…" He continued kissing her. Lips. Tongues. Hands. Exploring. Caressing. "Ken, I want you…"

The short-wave radio screeched.

"Son-of-a-bitch," he shouted. He didn't want to answer the radio. He wanted to make love to Toni. This was the only time they would be alone. On the other hand, guys at the command post knew they were together in the shelter. Gossip would be blowing faster than the windstorm. His body rendered the final decision. He couldn't make love to anyone now.

He got up and answered the radio.

"*Hai.*"

"Looks like the storm has stopped. Luckily you've only been trapped for half a day. As soon as the ski lifts are operable, we will come to rescue you. Do you need more than a stretcher?" Jun asked in Japanese.

"Yes," Kenji said. "Please send food. There is nothing here to eat except packages of ramen gnawed by mice. We're hungry. Also all emergency provisions in this shelter need to be restocked."

Kenji looked at Toni bracing herself up on her elbows, adjusting her sweater. She did not look happy to be rescued. For some reason he found her sad face endearing. He picked up their clothes warmed by the fire and shook them out.

"Our clothes are dry now. You can get

out of that dirty futon."

She looked at him with a shy smile.

"Toni, I think I'm falling in love with you. If your leg is okay, we can ski down to the bottom of the hill, get in my car and drive to the nearest airport. I was supposed to be skiing in St. Moritz this week anyway. Have you ever been to Switzerland?"

She shook her head. "The farthest I've ever been from the U.S. is Japan. The only places I ever skied are in Idaho and Utah. What do ski bums do in the summer? Do you even have a real job?"

"I get an allowance from my mother. I have a job waiting for me from my father. Money's no problem. Toni, I want to share the world with you. We can ski in the European Alps in the winter, sun on the Riviera and dive in the Caribbean. Have you ever been to Paris? We can cruise down the Seine at night under the glow of lights from the Eiffel Tower. We can watch bullfights in Madrid. I want you by my side forever."

She held his face in her hands. "Running away with you sounds exciting, but it's just an empty dream. If we had met each other in another time and place, our lives could have been different. But now, you have your brother's wedding next week, and I have my husband and kids to take care of. Any plans we make will be interrupted by real life. Like this radio."

SAVED BY THE BELL, or in this case, the short wave radio, Toni thought. _What was I thinking? I could have been raped—however, I wanted him to make love to me. I must be a terrible_

Lake Biwa Wishes

wanton woman. No man has ever made me feel so passionately wicked before. I need to get back to reality. I need to get my head back together. It's a good thing I'll never see Kenji Nakamura again.

Chapter Seventeen

Christmas Eve, 1976
Tokai-mura, Japan

"Today is the big day," Toni said to herself as she walked into the GE Guesthouse. She was on the planning committee for the employee Christmas party for the Japanese and American engineers. She knew that most Japanese were not Christians, so Christmas was party time rather than church and family time. Toni spent all week rehearsing with the American children of St. Mary's Academy branch. They were to be the main entertainment. Although Greg was not an employee of GE, Toni was the volunteer art and music teacher for the school's eight students. Two of the eight were their sons.

She checked out the sound equipment and tested the microphones in the large ballroom. While arranging decorations on the stage in the Christmas fairyland with artificial snow-covered trees, giant candy canes, and reindeer, she noticed with amusement that the larger-than-life-size Santa Claus looked more like a red-suited Japanese man with a glued on fluffy cotton beard.

Doors opened and guests swarmed in. The Japanese men wore suits, accompanied by their wives who looked beautiful in their brocaded silk kimonos. Toni was happy to see children with them. She was aware of how rare a family party was in Japan.

She passed out peppermint candy canes to the children—and one for herself. While sucking on a candy cane, she heard someone call "Morgan-san...Toni." She turned around. "Merry Christmas."

"Ken. What a nice surprise. Merry Christmas. What are you doing here?" She stuffed the rest of the candy in her mouth.

"Looking for you. I was driving through Tokai, and thought I'd stop by."

"Liar. Tokai is not on the road to anywhere. At least not anywhere you would go."

"Busted. I did want to see you though."

Lake Biwa Wishes

She looked at his puppy dog eyes, remembered his kisses, and got that fluttery feeling again. They were in public. People could see them. She hoped she wasn't blushing. *Say something.* "Would…would you like to join us?" she stammered. "The party just started."

"I'm not an employee."

"Neither is my husband. I'm here as the entertainment coordinator."

"I've never seen so many women and children at company parties," Kenji said as he looked around and nodded to the various guests.

"The Japanese men were told they were not welcomed unless they brought their wives and kids. No mistresses. This is a family party," she said.

Kenji grinned. "I'll bet you had something to do with that. Still trying to change the world? Your courage never fails to amaze me. Why are your kids in the American school? Aren't the Japanese public schools good enough?"

"Gaijin aren't allowed in Japanese public schools."

"Really? I didn't know that. I only attended private schools as a kid."

"It's a cultural thing, not the law. I haven't been able to change that tradition …yet."

Suddenly Toni felt someone tugging on her sleeve. "Mommy, the French kids are being mean to the Japanese kids again." She put her arm around him.

"This is my six-year-old, Danny. Danny,

this is Nakamura-san, my ski instructor."

"*Hajimemashite,*" her son said with a bow.

"Hajimemashite. I speak English, Danny."

"That's okay, I can speak Japanese. Did you teach my Mom to ski fast? We always have to wait for her on the ski hill."

"Your mother is a good skier. She's just afraid of the unknown."

"Ooooh, the unknown! Maybe I can scare the French kids."

"Just say to them, '*Vous êtes impoli. Arrête!*'" Kenji said.

"*Vous—impoli—Arrête!*" Danny said as he walked away.

"Your son is cute—looks like you."

"Thanks, but he'd be insulted if you said

he looked like a girl. My older son Roger, the nine-year-old with my guitar, wears his hair long and is often mistaken for a girl."

KENJI CHUCKLED. STANDING NEXT TO HER son was the only blond man in the room. _Must be Toni's husband._ Kenji could only see the back of his head, but it angered him to think Toni was that man's wife. Instead, he said, "Japanese men haven't caught up with the rest of the world on male fashion. People at the airport did a double take when they saw me not sporting a typical crew cut."

"What did you do?"

"Spoke English so they would think I was an American." Toni reacted with a giggle. It warmed his heart when he could make her laugh. He couldn't believe they were making small talk when he really wanted to take her in his arms. "Is your son an international peacemaker like you?"

"I'm afraid so. Danny cares about other people," she said. She furrowed her eyes. "I didn't know you spoke French."

"I asked you to come and live with me in Paris..."

"I didn't think you really meant live there. I thought you were looking for a travel playmate or just using a seductive line."

"No. I was serious about you. Still am."

She looked at him like she wanted to say something, but closed her mouth and smiled instead.

That warm mouth—he could almost taste it. Kenji didn't know how much longer he could stand there pretending she was just another gaijin acquaintance. He still wanted to run away with her—to the moon, if possible.

"Oh, I almost forgot. The real reason I came was to give you this. Merry Christmas," he said handing her a small festively wrapped package.

"*Domo arigato.* I wish I had known you were coming, I don't have a present for you."

"All I want is to see your face and know that I once meant something to you."

She couldn't help smiling. "You did and you still do. I only wish our situations were different." He mentally begged her to leave with him. "I love you, Toni," he mouthed silently.

He saw the angst on her face. He wanted to take her in his arms and make her laugh again. He felt like such a helpless fool, wanting her so badly, yet pretending to be a casual acquaintance.

"Ken, don't. You saw my two sons. They're my reality. I can't leave them."

What was I thinking? I came to Tokai to take Toni away with me, to be with me forever. But her husband and children are real. How could I live with myself knowing that a little boy somewhere would always think of Christmas as the day his mother ran away with another man? I'm not that kind of monster. Running away is a fantasy. I have to let her go—no matter how it hurts.

"Should I open my present now?" she asked.

"*Dozo.*"

She untied the red ribbon and opened the package wrapped Japanese style without tape. She looked up at him. "It's a Karen

Carpenter cassette. Thank you, Ken. She's my favorite. I'd kiss you, but I almost created a scandal kissing my husband."

"I heard about that," he said as he grinned. *I know your kiss. In fact, I'd kill for another one.* He watched her remove the plastic cover. "It's a karaoke tape. You have to sing to it. The printed words are in English and Japanese. It's…you know, our song."

"Oh, Ken, you're going to make me cry."

"Please don't. Americans hate tears. Sign of weakness they say." He drank in the sight of her biting her lower lip and thought his composure would collapse if he stayed any longer. "I just wanted to see you one last time. *Sayonara,* Toni-chan."

"Good-bye, Ken."

Lake Biwa Wishes

On his way out, he was stopped. *"Nakamura-san, Komban-wa."* The Mayor of Tokai recognized him and started up a conversation. He had no idea what the man was saying. Kenji's eyes were fixated on Toni walking away from him. He watched as she put the tape into the karaoke player. Kenji bowed politely to the mayor and hurried out the double doors of the GE Guesthouse, down the steps to his car. Music from the party was piped over the loudspeakers. He could hear Toni singing. He gripped the door handle when he heard *"...Just like me, they long to be close to you."*

Kenji got into his car and slammed his hands on the steering wheel. He wiped his eyes with the back of his hand and drove to Tokyo.

Chapter Eighteen

October 1983
San Francisco, California

"Toni...Toni Morgan?"

Toni turned around. "Ken Nakamura? What on earth are you doing in California?" She stopped while her friends were hurrying to the entrance of the Catholic Retreat Center. This was the last place she would ever expect to see Kenji, but there he was, sitting on a low rock wall facing the circle drive across from the building. Framed by the fall blooming chrysanthemums, he looked as handsome as she remembered. Dressed in a navy blue sport jacket atop tan slacks with no tie, he looked as comfortable in California as he did wearing ski clothes in Japan. He grinned at her with those sad puppy dog eyes she once found so sensual. His sex appeal hadn't faltered after all those years.

Since the weather was unseasonably warm for October, Toni and two friends had gone for a long walk during their afternoon break. "Toni, hurry up. The meeting already started," a man said, holding open one of the heavy wooden double doors.

"You guys go ahead and save me a seat. I'll be a little late." She turned to Kenji. "Are you living in the Bay Area now?"

He shook his head. "I had a business meeting in San Francisco. Do you live in California?

"No. We still live in Idaho. I fly back tomorrow afternoon." Seeing Kenji again was so unexpected. She set down her backpack and sat beside him.

IT HAD BEEN ALMOST SEVEN YEARS since he last saw her. She didn't seem older, just more charming. Her long hair was currently shoulder length and she wore makeup now, but he thought she looked as beautiful as ever.

"It's been a while. You look great," he said.

"Thanks. So do you. I can't believe bumping into you. What on earth are you doing at this Retreat Center?" she asked.

"My mother accompanied me on this trip. Since she's Catholic, she likes to meditate in these gardens and grounds. One of those men your husband?"

"No. I'm here for a church meeting. My husband hates church politics."

"You always have men around you. Doesn't he get jealous?"

"He'd better not. Until more women get elected to church leadership, I'll probably be in the minority. I believe in equality of the sexes."

"Still out to save the world?" he asked with a grin. She closed her eyes and nodded.

Just then a little boy walked over to join them. "*Otōsan...*"

"This is my son, Ryoichi," Kenji said as he presented the child to Toni. He turned to his son and said, "*Kochira wa Morgan-san.*"

"*Konnichi-wa Ryoichi-san,*" she said to the boy who seemed to be about five or six.

"I'm fine. Pleased to meet you, Morgan-san," he said.

"You speak perfect English. And you're just as handsome as your father." Ryoichi tried to keep a straight face, but broke into a toothless grin.

"Father, may I go play near the gardens? Grandmother is there."

"Yes, but stay where one of us can see you," Kenji said.

"He's a cute, well-behaved little boy."

"Ryoichi is the light of my life. I never understood the close relationship between my brother and father until I had a son of my own. He is my first born—a continuation of my existence."

"Is his mother here with you? Did you finally marry Mariko?"

"Mariko?" He thought for a moment. *Who's Mariko?* Then he remembered. Her elusive friend. He grinned. "You're kidding, of course. After my brother's wedding I went back to Boulder instead of St. Moritz." He hesitated for a moment. "I couldn't get you out of my head, so I packed up and returned to Tokyo. My mother arranged for me to meet someone she thought was a good match. I married a woman named Reiko."

SHE COULDN'T BELIEVE SHE WAS sitting here with him. *Was he still attracted to her after all these years?* She knew she still felt that tingle of excitement being near him.

"When I saw you that Christmas, I intended to give you an ultimatum to leave your husband, or I would marry Reiko. Meeting you face to face, I realized my attempt was stupid, so I got married anyway."

"You were going to give me an ultimatum? What do you think would have happened if you did?"

A wide grin spread across his face. "We would have had a knock-down-drag-out fight right on the dance floor and people would have learned new American euphemisms."

"We are just too incompatible." She laughed. "So tell me, what is your wife like?"

"Reiko is a good wife and mother. I respect her. We're expecting another baby in four months."

"How exciting. Are you traveling

around the world together?"

"No. Reiko hates to travel. She doesn't want to leave Japan. When Ryoichi is older, I'll take him around the world with me."

She shook her head. "Are you happy?"

"I now work for my father's newspaper and I'm a respectable member of our company—a salary-man and a family man."

She looked into his eyes. "You don't sound very happy, Ken."

"And you still don't mince words." He gave her that half grin which she once found so sexy. "I miss your outspokenness."

"Ken, where's your son?" Toni's maternal instincts kicked in. "California's not as safe as Japan, you know." They got up from the wall seat to look for the boy.

"Ryoichi!" Kenji called out.

"*Hai.*" They found him playing on the grass in front of the labyrinth where his grandmother was walking and praying.

"See, he's safe. It's not like he's lost in a snowstorm," he said with a twinkle in his eye.

She let the intended meaning of his comment slide by. "There are more dangers here than in Japan, like kidnappers and muggers, molesters..."

"...and lions and tigers and bears," he added. "Aha!"

She giggled. She noticed his eyes focused on someone behind her.

"My mother has completed praying the labyrinth. Would you like to meet her?"

Toni nodded, although she was apprehensive about meeting Kenji's mother. She felt like the "other woman," even though she'd done nothing wrong. His mother was not as she envisioned. Mrs. Nakamura was tall, beautiful—belying her age—and she spoke English. When Kenji introduced them and mentioned that they met on a ski hill in Lake Biwa, her eyes flashed.

"How did you enjoy living in our country?"

"It was one of the highlights of my life. In fact, my husband and I divide our lives into before and after living in Japan."

"You are delightful, my child..." A nun approached them.

"Mrs. Nakamura, the meeting room with the Japanese woodprints is now vacant. Please come and see how we exhibited the artwork you donated."

Toni watched them walk away, and

then turned her attention back to Kenji.

She took his hand. "It's been fun talking to you again, Ken. I have to get back to the meeting."

He hesitated for a moment. "Toni, can I see you later tonight—when your meeting is over?"

"Kenji Nakamura, are you asking me for a date?"

"Of course not. Why? Do you usually date other men?"

"No. What kind of woman do you think I am? I'm just teasing you." She noticed his suggestive half grin. "Now, don't go calling me names. We're in a convent."

"Seriously. Can I pick you up somewhere? Maybe we can go for dinner in town and talk."

Lake Biwa Wishes

"Will your mother and son join us?"

"No. They go to bed early."

"Then yes." Toni did want to spend more time with him—as an old friend. "Pick me up at seven, in the curved driveway in front of the Center."

Chapter Nineteen

That evening Kenji drove up in his rented black Cadillac. He waited for a few minutes then saw Toni rush out of the building. He got out of the car and opened the passenger door for her.

"Sorry I'm late. I tried calling Greg but couldn't reach him. The kids said he was still at work. I called his office, but missed him. Must have been on the road."

Lake Biwa Wishes

"You know what they say—when the cat's away..." He snickered.

She shook her head. "Greg's not like that."

"Where would you like to go?"

"How about the Grotto Bay House? It's nearby with a beautiful view of the bay."

He drove as she directed, across US-101 and eventually onto a lonely gravel road in a secluded area. The restaurant was large with a panoramic view of the San Francisco Bay. She knows her way around here, he thought. He remembered she said she was from Idaho.

After being told there was an hour wait for a table at the restaurant, they walked to the adjoining cocktail lounge decorated with heavy ropes and nets with colorful float globes hanging from the walls. He squinted at the lighted floor to ceiling wall of liquor bottles. "There's a table in the corner where we could talk." They sat at the square thick hewn table large enough for two. The waitress came and he ordered two beers. "I can't believe we're sitting here together. I thought I would never see you again. Must be fate," he said. The waitress brought their beers and poured the foamy liquid into their goblets. "So what have you been doing since you left Japan?" he asked after savoring his Coors.

"Greg and I traveled to Korea and China before we came home. Then as opportunities opened up, I joined the work force at the Idaho Lab."

"What did you do?"

"I worked as a systems engineer, and climbed   the   organization   ladder   into engineering management." He raised his eyebrows. "My degrees were in Engineering. When I graduated from college, no one would hire women engineers, but things are different now."

"Impressive. Do you still sing?"

"Just church choir stuff." She pressed her lips together. "I still have that karaoke tape you gave me—kinda wore it out, especially after Karen Carpenter died."

"I liked hearing you sing." He downed the rest of his beer and ordered two more, picking up the empty bottle and examining the label. "Can't get Coors in Japan. I really miss it—as well as other American things." He looked into her eyes. "I never forgot our short time together. Do you ever think of me?"

"I think of you whenever I go skiing.

You were my best ski instructor."

"Do you ski often?"

She sipped more beer. "My older son Roger is on the ski team, so we spend weekends at competitions. After doing the cheerleader mom thing, I try to get in a few runs."

"I mean do you ever think of *me*? I was so crazy in love with you I was tempted to kidnap you."

She slammed down her glass, making the liquid swirl. "Well, you certainly didn't waste any time getting over me. You got married and had a baby before I even left Japan, by my calculations." She picked up her glass and downed the rest of her beer.

"You rejected me. I was so pissed at you I took it out on Reiko and married her. I've been trying to make it up to her ever since."

The waitress brought two fresh bottles of beer. Toni refilled his glass. Kenji topped off her glass. They were friends again.

"You know I couldn't run away with you that night. I had my family. Would you leave your son and pregnant wife if I begged you to run away with me right now?"

"Depends. How hard would you beg?"

"I'm not kidding." She swatted his arm. "Ken, when I stand at the top of a ski hill looking at the vista below, I feel your arms around me, guiding me around and over the moguls. I think of you whenever I hear 'our song.' And I think of you when..." She couldn't continue. Just then two members of her church committee walked in. She nodded at them.

"Are you going to the party later tonight?" one man asked.

"Probably not. We haven't had dinner yet," she said.

They sat in silence for a few minutes. Finally he asked, "Are you really attending a church meeting, or partying with those guys?"

"It's not what it sounds like. We usually get together to strategize on certain issues. We don't really party. I'm giving you the wrong impression of myself."

What was she? A church matron? A party girl? He never had enough time to get to know her well. "So when *do* you think of me? When you're having ball-busting sex?"

She furrowed her eyebrows. "Where did you learn that kind of language?"

Lake Biwa Wishes

"Not from experience," he said, pulling the loose Coors label off his bottle.

"Are you still Kenji the womanizer, or did married life slow you down? My sixteen-year-old Roger plays the guitar, and being on the ski team, I can't keep girls away from him. He reminds me of you instead of his father." She took another sip of her beer.

"You made up the womanizer label. In Colorado, I was the nerdy Japanese foreign student. Only skiing and blond snow bunnies made me look cool. Inside, I'm still the nerd, and I'm still...fascinated by you." He covered her hand. "Now what were you going to say before you were interrupted?"

"Sometimes I think of you when I'm alone on travel in some hotel room, and I have fantasies..."

"Like tonight?"

She sighed. "No, thank goodness. I'm staying in a convent."

"What's it like?"

"The guest rooms are small, with a single bed, a table and chair, and a sink. No locks on the doors. Communal showers and toilets down the hall. The men are assigned to one floor, the women to another floor, and the nuns to a third. We are all kept apart at a safe distance."

"We could go to my hotel," he said not looking directly at her.

"You want a one night stand with me?"

"I'll take anything I can get."

"You certainly won't get anything if you insult me like that."

He rolled his eyes. "What the hell did I

say now? You are impossible."

"If all you want is sex, I'm sure your hotel has lists of call girls. You could even pick up a girl at any bar."

"I don't want a call girl. In fact, I don't know why I ever wanted you."

"Me too. I'm glad you married your compliant little Reiko. She deserves a jerk like you."

"And I'm glad you didn't leave your super stud *hakujin*."

"You mean my husband? His name is Greg."

"Whatever…"

"Morgan. Not whatever."

"Do you fight with everybody?"

She calmed down and said, "Only with you. Other people know better than to mess with me."

"Suddenly I feel like the nerdy foreign student again," he said, shaking his head.

"If I bleach my hair blond and snowplow down the bunny hill, will you look cool?" He broke into a full laugh.

The maître d' announced their table was ready. They walked to a coveted table next to the window as Kenji gently put his hand on the curve of her back. When they were seated, he said, "I'm sorry I offended you, Toni. No one night stand for us. I don't want to lose your friendship. Who would I have to fight with?"

"Your wife?"

"She barely talks to me. She always agrees with me. If I get mad at her, she retreats into herself. Her way of making me feel guilty."

"It's always all about you? Maybe she's the miserable one having to put up with a conceited husband." He looked at her, then shrugged one shoulder.

"What about *you*? You badmouth a woman you don't even know then turn around and defend her with your life."

She looked down at her menu. "Yeah, I guess I do that."

"That's what attracts me to you."

"I thought you were attracted by my sexy bod," she said as she winked her eye.

"We won't discuss that until I get a napkin on my lap."

"...at least I'm not racist," she continued.

"I apologize for that also. I don't hate white men. I'm just jealous of *him*."

She bit her lip. She still felt the magnetism between them, even after all these years. "I'm sorry I sounded mean. My feelings were hurt to know you married *her* days after you begged me to run away with you."

He meant to hurt her. He was so impetuous in those days. He ended up hurting himself more. "You asked if I was happy. Are you?" he asked.

"Yes."

"Any regrets?"

"From time to time. You were the one who taught me that falling down is part of practice. Regrets are part of living. I enjoy my life." A waiter brought her order of steamed black cod wrapped in origami. She lifted the paper cover and closed her eyes while sniffing the aroma of spiced soy sauce covering the fish.

Kenji watched, enjoying her reaction to the food while she took a bite. Strange, how he could get turned on simply by watching her eat fish. He sliced into his steak and they ate silently, sneaking glances at each other.

"The cod is delicious," she said as she pierced a piece with her fork and offered it to him. He opened his mouth and held onto the fork with his lips, letting her slowly pull it away.

"Have a taste of my meat," he said as he sliced a bite of steak to feed her. He didn't realize the act of sharing food could be so sexually arousing.

She put down her fork. "Ken, I asked you before—are you happy?"

"I guess so. I'm not a jet-setting kid

anymore. I'm contented now."

"What's your typical day like?"

He closed his eyes and sighed. "Like everyone else. I get up in the morning, go to work, attend meetings, return home, relax in my bath, have dinner, go to bed, and repeat the whole routine the next day."

"Sounds really boring," she said as she pointed her forefinger into her open mouth.

"This is the life fate had in store for me."

"Bullshit!"

"Toni, I thought all this church stuff made you a religious person." He couldn't help chuckling.

"It's not your fate to become a dull, hollow old man. The Kenji I knew cared about people. You carried me on your back through a snowstorm. You shed tears worrying about our friends. The old Kenji was passionate, whether teaching, skiing, loving, or tempting me with stories about worldly adventures."

He pushed his empty plate aside. He couldn't look at her. She was right. He felt dull and hollow.

"Okay, your turn for a smart ass retort."

"You're right," he said. "I was getting bored—almost to the point of depression. Playing with Ryoichi saved my sanity, but you're right. He will grow up. You laugh at my belief in fate, but you seem to show up in my life whenever I need you."

SHE LOOKED AT HIM, SURPRISED. She expected another fight. He was somber—pensive to the extent of looking sexier than with his half-grin. It was a good thing they were in public. She wanted him badly.

"You know I got bent out of shape by that one-night-stand comment because I would never cheat on my husband. I promised to love him until I died. Besides, if he found out, he would be sad, forgive me, and blame himself. That's just how he is. I could never forgive myself."

He chuckled quietly.

"You think that's funny?"

"Only because Reiko is the same way. She even implied that she wouldn't mind if I had a mistress. But I couldn't two-time any woman, especially my wife."

I thought he was a womanizing playboy. He's not. Maybe that's why I can't forget him. We only knew each other for a few days. I wish situations could have been different between us, but

Lake Biwa Wishes

we can still be good friends—friends without benefits.

Chapter Twenty

Outside, they strolled along the lighted path overlooking the bay. Toni shivered in the evening air, so Kenji took off his jacket and put it around her shoulders. They walked to the bridge leading to Woolley Park where they could see lights from the boats on the bay as well as airplanes taking off and landing at the San Francisco Airport. He put his arm protectively around her. She turned and kissed him on the cheek. He was surprised, but didn't want to let her go. Ever.

"Ken, I love you—as a friend—and I want you to enjoy life. Fate isn't involved. You have to make an effort to be happy. When was the last time you went skiing with your buddies—not company trips, but with people you really care about?"

He silently looked at their reflection in the water.

"You don't have to wait for your wife—go by yourself. Please don't waste the rest of your life blaming me. And don't give Ryoichi a guilt complex if he will prefer chasing girls to being with his old man. I have teenagers, and neither of them would be caught dead with their parents."

He pulled her back to him. "I wish

things could be different with us. We would make good sparing partners as well as lovers."

He stood on the bridge with her, never wanting to let her go. They stood there in silence, listening to the airplanes take off.

"I almost forgot." He pulled out a small blue velvet box. She opened it and found a pendant of tiny gold skis connected by two diamonds.

"Oh Ken, it's beautiful. As usual, I don't have anything for you."

"That's okay. I saw this in a jewelry store and thought of you." He put the pendant on her, then kissed the back of her neck.

"Are you cold?" he asked.

"No, I have your jacket. Are you cold?"

"I've got your love to keep me warm."

"If you think I'm going to break into a

song now, you're crazy."

He laughed and held her close. "Toni, can I see you off at the airport tomorrow?"

"Why? Are we going to enact a going-to-war scene and slobber over each other?"

"That would be great, but I'll take anything I can get."

"Okay, but only chaste goodbye kisses. Not like this…"

"Good god, Toni," he said when they stopped to take a breath. "You're still a PT. I'm craving a one-night stand, or two nights, or every night for the rest of my life."

She hugged him. "We'd better get back. The Center has a curfew. And yes, you may see me off at the airport. I'll give you my flight information when we get to the car."

The next day Kenji waited with her at the San Francisco airport, sitting at Starbuck's, drinking coffee. He recognized one of the men on her committee. "Do these men traveling with you wonder about seeing us together?"

"No one has said anything to me. They probably think you're a relative. In addition to not having enough women as church leaders, there aren't many Asian Americans. Idahoans assume I know every Asian person in the world," she said with a grimace.

"Yeah, I get the same reaction from white people." He blew on his hot coffee.

She looked down at his hand. "Ken, how come you don't wear a wedding ring? Do you pretend to be single on business trips?"

He grinned. "Reiko and I had a Shinto wedding. We didn't exchange wedding bands."

"Well then, I have something for you." She handed him a small box which he immediately opened.

"It's a jade ring. Does this mean we're married now?" he said.

"Of course not. It's a friendship ring. The jade is Chinese, but the gold around it is American."

"Just like you."

"You now have something to remember me by."

"When did you have time to buy a ring? I took you back to the Center pretty late last night."

"I have a cousin who's a jeweler in San

Francisco. He brought several choices this morning. If it doesn't fit, you can have it re-sized." She put it on his finger. It fit perfectly.

"Thank you." He kissed her cheek.

"Let's wait until the plane loads. Then you can thank me appropriately."

Chapter Twenty-One

May 1988
Idaho Falls, Idaho

Toni stood in the doorway of the Presbyterian Church, receiving hugs and sympathy. The church was filled to capacity. She wanted to personally thank the friends who gathered to pay homage to Greg's life. Greg would have been pleased to see so many people. *Maybe he was up there somewhere watching.*

It wasn't until the service ended that Toni realized she was a widow. *A widow? That was an old lady, not someone her age. Like old Widow Smith, whom the kids brought cookies to every Christmas.*

The reception in the fellowship hall seemed more like a party than a funeral. For a few minutes, she took mental notes to share with Greg about what he missed, but he was never coming back.

Everything happened so fast. The scene flashed through her mind like a cheap movie. She relived step by step that day he died. She got a phone call that Greg had collapsed during a workplace meeting. By the time she drove to the hospital to meet the ambulance, the doctors said they couldn't save him. She hadn't known Greg had a bad heart. But then since they returned from Japan, they had little time for each other. After Toni joined the laboratory workforce, both she and Greg traveled a lot.

She didn't cry. She couldn't breathe. The lump in her throat was so thick, and her eyes hurt, but the tears wouldn't come. Couldn't come.

She looked at her sons. Neither Roger nor Danny was crying. They seemed like robots, with smiles plastered on their faces, shaking hands with friends.

Her neighbor, Marcia, brought her a hot cup of coffee. "What are you going to do about your planned trip to Japan? Were you able to get reimbursed?"

Toni took a sip. The Presbyterian plasma was too hot as usual. She burned her tongue. "I got my trip changed to open reservations. I still want to travel. If I stay here, I'll just get depressed. Maybe Roger or Danny will go with me. My friend Midori invited me to stay at her home," Toni said.

Greg's office mate, John, joined them. "So sorry about Greg. You know I'll do anything to help you, Toni."

"I'll leave you two to talk. Someone needs my help at the refreshment table," Marcia said as she left.

"Thanks, John. I'll need your help to collect his personal things from his office…"

They heard loud sobbing from across the room. Three women were standing together. One kept wiping her eyes. "Who are those women?" she asked John.

"Two of them are young engineers Greg was mentoring. I don't know who the third woman is."

"I never knew Greg was in the mentoring business."

John raised his eyebrows and pretended to smile.

"Was that what Greg was doing while I was traveling on all those church and business trips?"

"No comment. It's rude to speak ill of the dead," John replied.

All these years I thought I was a happily married woman. Wasn't Greg happy? I wonder.

Chapter Twenty-Two

The following Monday, Toni went to Greg's office to pick up his personal possessions. She couldn't believe that Greg had been unfaithful to her. Her emotions flipped between sadness and anger. *How could he do this to me? I thought we were the perfect couple. Evidently he didn't think I was enough for him.* She pulled into the parking lot so quickly she almost hit a parked vehicle.

Lake Biwa Wishes

She stayed in her car to regain her composure before facing the security guard. The signs were all there. She just didn't realize it until now. When she traveled, there were the calls home that went unanswered which she attributed to his work dedication. Then the bills from his travels increased. She had wondered why he didn't include them on his lab expense account. *Were there many other women? Or did Greg really love someone else?*

She finally got out of her car, smoothed her skirt, and walked to the building showing her badge to the security guard. "My condolences on your loss," the guard said. Toni nodded.

When she got to Greg's office, John was already piling cardboard boxes on the work table.

"Hi, Toni. I'm almost through packing. I'll help you carry the boxes to your car."

She looked around the room. It seemed strange not to see Greg working on his computer. She touched the desk and unconsciously wiped the dust away. "So how long has Greg been cheating on me?"

"Huh? Toni, I just shared an office with him. I didn't know his deep dark secrets."

"Well, I shared a bed with him, and I never knew his deep dark secrets either." Suddenly she felt an ache in her chest. She sat before Greg's computer. "What happens to this computer?"

"Our boss said I was to send it to Archives. His research is in those files."

Also his emails. She sat down and began typing. "Who's Michele? Greg had lots of emails with her."

"She was one of the girls he mentored. The other girl is named Rocky."

"You're kidding."

He chuckled. "Guess her real name is Raquel or something."

"Who's Amy?"

"No idea. There's no one named Amy in our department."

She searched Greg's email files. Correspondence with Amy went back five years. Some of the notes were explicitly personal. Toni was surprised Greg kept them on his work computer. She found several lunch and dinner dates planned for when she was out of town.

She stopped typing. "I wish Greg was still here." Tears began running down her face.

"Me, too," John said.

Toni slammed her hands on the keyboard. The screen lit up with a smattering of type like so many bad words.

She shouted, "I want Greg to be alive right now so I could kill the bastard!"

John put his arm around her. "What's past is past. Besides, we really don't know what happened. Toni, don't do this to yourself. You're still young, pretty, an accomplished woman. Maybe you'll find someone better."

"Right now I'm through with *all* men."

Chapter Twenty-Three

June 1988
Japan

As it turned out, neither son could travel at the same time as Toni's vacation from her job. She thought, I've traveled alone before, and I can still speak a little Japanese. _I have to learn to be independent now._

Toni exchanged her two airline tickets for one in first class and set out for Japan three weeks later. After connecting through Salt Lake City and Los Angeles, she boarded the Tokyo bound flight early and sat in her window seat sipping a complimentary glass of champagne.

A businessman sat in the adjoining seat. He asked, "Are you traveling on business?"

"Not this time. My husband and I had planned a trip to Japan, but he recently died."

"Oh, I'm sorry. Please accept my condolence." He quickly busied himself reading his reports.

Toni had been warned by older women that when their husbands died, friends avoided them, not knowing what to say after "I'm sorry." She wasn't offended. She probably reacted the same way in the past. *I refuse to be a simpering widow. Greg wasn't worth it.*

Lake Biwa Wishes

After waiting in long lines at customs and immigration, she finally got her luggage and rolled it into the main terminal. Narita Airport appeared the same as when she left Tokyo, only bigger, brighter and noisier. She looked up at the expansiveness of the open balcony filled with restaurants and shops and almost missed Midori and Hiro waving to her. She wanted to hug them but got all confused about whether to embrace them or bow. She bowed.

Even though they had exchanged photos over the years, she noted that Hiro was grayer around the temples and Midori had put on a little weight. But she still had that captivating smile.

"Welcome back to Japan," Hiro said. "Sorry about Greg-san. We will miss him."

Midori silently held Toni's hands, blinking back her tears.

"Thank you for picking me up. I should have taken the train. It's a long drive."

"You are our guest, and we want the privilege of delivering you to our home ourselves. Other friends wanted to meet you at the airport, but we convinced them to wait at our house. Too many cars make too much traffic," Hiro said.

Toni remembered the first day she had arrived in Japan twelve years ago. Narita Airport wasn't even built. Three company cars were waiting at Haneda Airport for the American Morgan family. The adults and two children were squished into one car and their luggage filled up the other two cars. It seemed like only yesterday, but Tokyo had changed a lot from those days, she noticed through the car window.

Hiro drove them to his new house in Ibaraki City. Like the other scientists and engineers, he had moved his family out of the cramped 1970s company housing in Tokai to a large house on a spacious suburban lot. The entire house was furnished and decorated in European style with accommodation for house guests.

Toni planned to wash up and take a rest after the long flight and car ride. However, when they arrived at the Tanaka's house, wall to wall people were there to welcome her. Men who worked with Greg, women who socialized with Toni, and even some of the kids Roger and Danny played with—all grown up now. She put on a smile, trying hard not to weep. She knew that the Japanese people would cry with her—they had too much empathy.

After Toni exchanged bows and shook hands with several old friends, Midori said, "I have a surprise for you. Turn around." Toni turned and almost bumped into Kenji Nakamura.

"Ken, what are you doing here?"

"I was invited. I didn't crash the party." He took her hand. "Please accept my condolences. I'm sorry for your loss." She glanced down at his hand and noticed he wore the ring she had given him years ago.

"Thank you, Ken. I'm really surprised to see you here. How's your family?"

"My son Ryoichi is eleven now and attends a private school. He pulled a photo out of his wallet. This is my daughter, Kyoko. She's almost five years old."

"Oh Ken, she's beautiful. You're so lucky to have a daughter. How's your wife?"

He took a deep breath. "She died two years ago. Cancer."

"I'm so sorry." Toni didn't know what else to say.

They walked outside onto the back deck which overlooked rice paddies on the next property. The sun was beginning to set over the hills in the distance.

"You must have been devastated."

"I was, but I worked through my grief and survived. You will too, eventually."

"Do you want to tell me about her?"

"Losing Reiko was hard. On her last day, I apologized for not loving her. She looked at me like she didn't understand. She forced a weak smile and said, 'Thank you for being my husband and giving me two beautiful children.' Then she died staring at the ceiling. I gently closed her eyes. I should never have married her. Someone else would have loved her and treated her better. I was so selfish—I married her out of spite."

Toni couldn't believe it. *After all these years, he's still blaming me?* But then, poor Kenji had lost his spouse. She was beginning to understand how that felt. "Ken I don't plan on being blamed for Reiko's life or death. But I think she understood. You were a good husband to her."

He looked at her, puzzled. "How would you know?"

"Did you beat her?"

"I'm not a violent man. I would never hit a woman."

"Did you have a mistress?

"No, of course not."

"Did you carouse with other women?"

"No. But I often imagined being with you, instead of her." He avoided her eyes.

"You can't be blamed for your thoughts as long as you didn't act on them. Reiko was probably better off than some of the women at this party. _Keno-san_ used to get a new set of dishes each time we girls visited her because she threw her dishes at her husband whenever she found out he had an affair. Do you remember my friend Akiko? She divorced her husband after we visited her beach house and she found another woman's clothes in her closets. She moved with her daughter to

Australia. *Suzuki-san* used to wear sunglasses and large hats. That usually happened after her husband came home drunk at night. And there are a few women in the next room who just accept their husbands' dalliances and pretend they have a happy marriage." *Yeah, like me.* "Reiko was fortunate to have you. You did love her in your own Japanese way."

"Maybe you're right," he said, as he leaned on the railing of the back lanai.

"You better believe I am. At least you had a chance to say goodbye to her. Greg just died without any warning. I know it's not his fault, but I was so infuriated with him. How do you fight with a dead man? I'm a monster."

Toni started crying so hard she couldn't stop. The dam she carefully held together finally burst. She was shaking so violently, all she could do was hold onto Kenji who had his arms around her. "Greg never even said goodbye to me…"

"It's okay, Toni. Cry it all out. Get mad at me if you need to. Yell. Scream. Hit me—I'm here for you." He stepped back and spread out his arms. Toni began beating his chest with her fists, then slowed down, sobbing between hiccups. He caressed her, putting his chin on top of her head. "Feel better? You can have me to fight with any time, any place. I'm here for you."

Toni blinked away tears when she noticed people inside the house watching through the window, slowly shaking their heads or dabbing their eyes with handkerchiefs. *Damn. I didn't want the event to be a pity party.*

As if he could read her mind, Kenji said, "You're still grieving. You're expected to cry. Don't be embarrassed."

"Oh Ken, I'm so glad you're here." She pulled away from him. "Walk me to the bathroom. I need to clean up my face."

After Toni regained her composure and accepted condolences from more friends, she sat down with Kenji again. "How did you know I was coming to Japan?"

He gave her his sexy half grin. "Midori told me."

"Since when did you and Midori become friends?"

"It's a long story. We bumped into each other—literally—while I was on ski patrol at Hakuba in Nagano. I asked about you and she said you both exchanged greeting cards at

Christmas. One day she shared all the letters and photos you had sent. Then after that, every New Year's she invited me up here and let me read your letters."

"Did she know about... us?"

"She'd never say if she did, but I suspect she had some kind of women's intuition."

"Ken it's just like you to know all about me and keep your life hidden. I assume you're skiing again, now that you're single?"

"Actually, after we met in California, I got together with some of my old ski buddies and we skied in Grenoble that winter. We've been meeting in a different country every year for a reunion. You brought me back to life that day. I'm eternally grateful."

"It pained me to see you—the passionate dreamer—hiding behind a placid façade. I would have beaten it off you at that point," she said.

"Like you did earlier? You sure can pack a punch for such a little... I mean 'petite' woman."

"As long as you don't call me a PT anymore."

He looked into her eyes. "Maybe you can stop being one now."

Chapter Twenty-Four

They rose from the sofa and lined up at the dinner buffet table. "Midori said this is called *Vygingu style* in Japanese," Toni commented.

He laughed. "*Vygingu style* is a cognate for Viking style which is easier for the Japanese to pronounce instead of smorgasbord." They took their food laden plates back out to the deck. Kenji pulled out a chair for Toni at a table with two other friends. The woman admired his jade ring.

"It was a gift from an old friend," he said. He noticed the concerned look on Toni's face. "I've never taken it off since the first day it was put on my finger." After more conversation, the other couple excused themselves and left to replenish their plates. He looked at her questioning eyes. "When I go on business trips, it keeps marauding women from hitting on me."

"Ken you are still as conceited as ever. Who would hit on you?"

"One woman did—changed my life forever."

She lifted a pendant from inside her blouse. _The diamond skis._ He beamed. "How did you know I would be here?"

"I didn't. It reminds me I can conquer all fears. A ski instructor once drilled that into my head."

"Must have been an excellent teacher."

"The best, although conceited." She laughed. The first time since Greg died.

"See, you still know how to laugh." Kenji took a drink of his beer. "How long will you be in Japan?"

"Just a week. I have two sons in college and one income now, so my job is a necessity."

"I can help you with their tuition and expenses. Money is no object," he said.

"What would I have to give you in return?"

He avoided looking at her. "My daughter needs a mother. She has no memory of Reiko like Ryoichi does…"

"You want me to be your daughter's nanny?" she asked with eyes wide open.

He shook his head. "No. I want you to be my wife. I'm trying to ask you in my clumsy way to marry me. Damn. I feel like a nerdy foreign student again."

"Ken, my husband just died," she whispered.

"Well, I didn't mean this instant. Whenever you feel you're ready. I can wait. I've already waited a lifetime—almost. I just want to put in my bid before all the other men flock to your door."

"At my age, men aren't flocking to my door, only birds."

"Good. I don't want to waste my time fighting off rivals. And I do get jealous, especially where you're concerned." He sprinkled leftover rice crumbs on the deck rail for the birds. Two bright blue Japanese robins swooped up the morsels.

"If I lived with you, married or not, we would be fighting all the time," she said.

He chuckled. "So what? If we can love as passionately as we fight, life will be worth living. I still want to take you to Paris, Madrid, and all the other places I promised. Will you marry me? Or at least keep company with me until you're ready?"

"Are you asking me to date you?"

"Yes. The amount of time I was able to spend with you was sporadic, to say the least. I want more of you—much more. Maybe now we can get our lives in sync."

"I've had fantasies of running away with you since I first met you. We're both single now. I'm willing to try," she said softly.

"You still didn't answer my question. Will you marry me?"

She hesitated for a moment, and then nodded. "I will. Can we seal it with a kiss?

"Nope. We're still in Japan with a crowd of people watching us. Once I get you alone, though…" he said with his sexy half grin.

"Promise, promises…"

"Hey, I always keep my promises, even if it takes years." He looked at her. His irresistible puppy dog eyes held her heart captive–again. "This is my fate. To be with you."

Toni smiled. *My Lake Biwa wishes have come true.*

The End (or the Beginning)

Author's Note:

I hope you have enjoyed reading my story about Toni and Kenji. My next book, *The Second Time Around... A New Man, A New Land, A New Plan,* will take them from Japan to Idaho and back to Japan in dealing with blended family relationships and adjusting to cross-cultural differences.

I would love to hear from you. Contact me via my publisher sursumcordapress@comcast.net.

Judy Lussie began writing fiction after her retirement as the Technical Information Department Head from Lawrence Livermore National Laboratory (LLNL). Her love of reading and church activities led to her being asked to write devotionals for *These Days Magazine*.

Originally from Chicago, Judy lived in Idaho for thirty years, with a two-year-stint in Japan, and relocated to California to work at the LLNL.

Her short stories have been included in the CWC Tri-Valley Branch's anthologies, *Voices of the Valley: The First Press, Encore* and *Word for Word*. Other short stories have been included in *Between Pages*; the Las Positas College Anthology, *Sparks*; and in *Word Movers*, an anthology of Creative Writings by Seniors, Oakland, CA.